MAYA
makes a
MESS

A TOON BOOK BY
RUTU MODAN

For Hilel,
who can never have too much pasta.

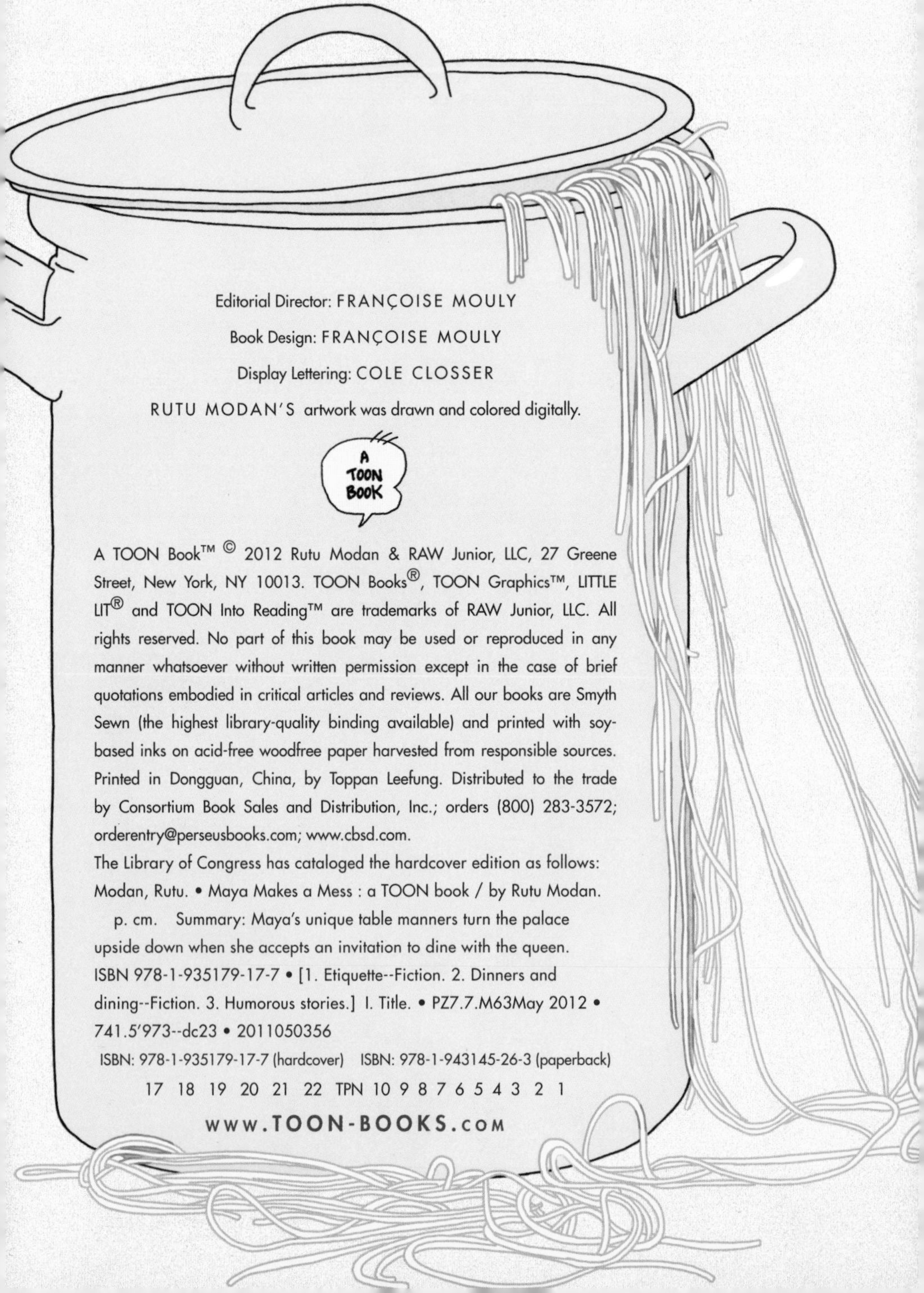

Editorial Director: FRANÇOISE MOULY

Book Design: FRANÇOISE MOULY

Display Lettering: COLE CLOSSER

RUTU MODAN'S artwork was drawn and colored digitally.

A TOON BOOK

 All our books are Smyth Sewn (the highest library-quality binding available) and printed with soy-based inks on acid-free woodfree paper harvested from responsible sources. Printed in Dongguan, China, by Toppan Leefung. Distributed to the trade by Consortium Book Sales and Distribution, Inc.; orders (800) 283-3572; orderentry@perseusbooks.com; www.cbsd.com.

The Library of Congress has cataloged the hardcover edition as follows:
Modan, Rutu. • Maya Makes a Mess : a TOON book / by Rutu Modan.
p. cm. Summary: Maya's unique table manners turn the palace upside down when she accepts an invitation to dine with the queen.
ISBN 978-1-935179-17-7 • [1. Etiquette--Fiction. 2. Dinners and dining--Fiction. 3. Humorous stories.] I. Title. • PZ7.7.M63May 2012 • 741.5'973--dc23 • 2011050356

ISBN: 978-1-935179-17-7 (hardcover) ISBN: 978-1-943145-26-3 (paperback)

17 18 19 20 21 22 TPN 10 9 8 7 6 5 4 3 2 1

www.TOON-BOOKS.com

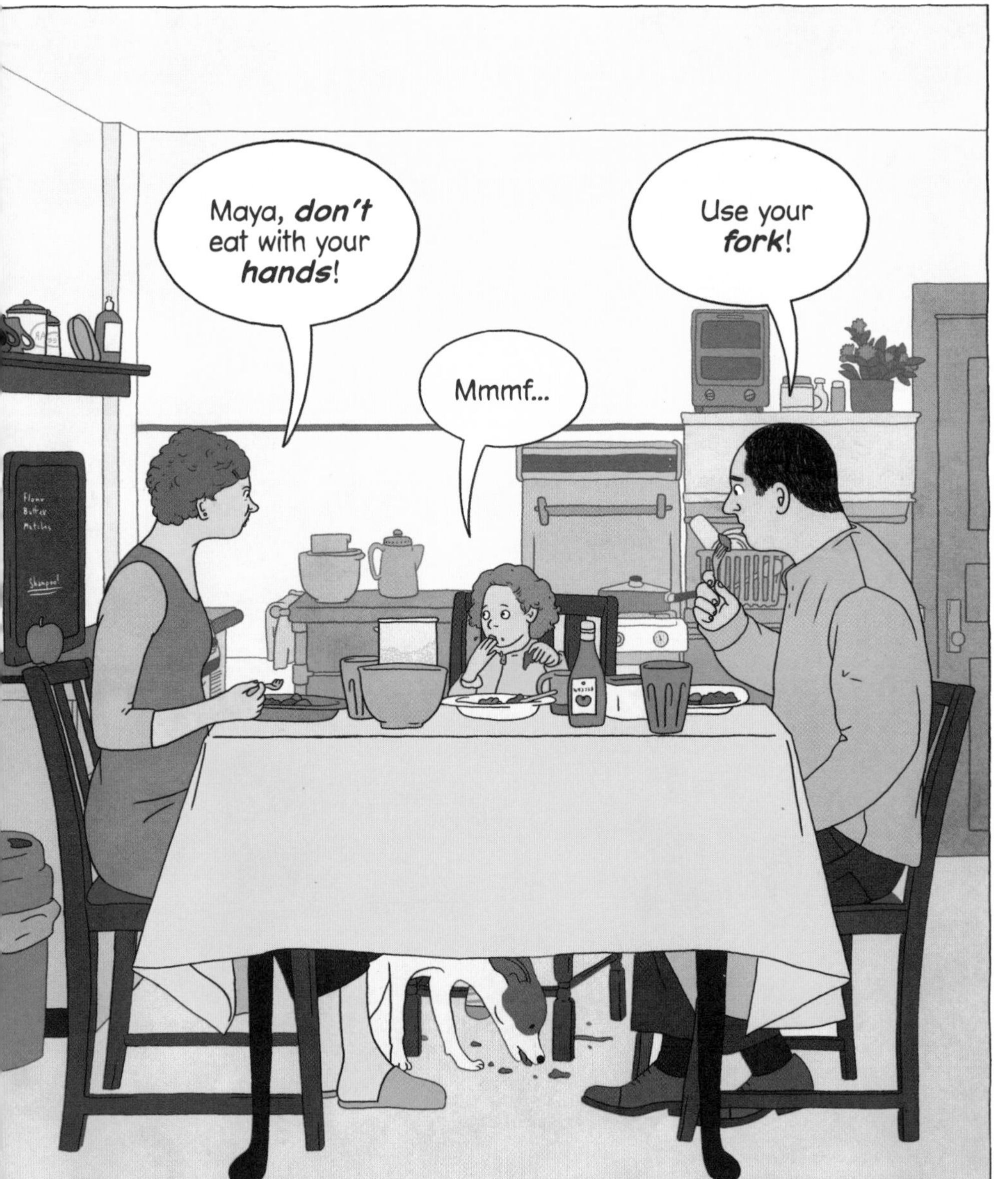
Maya, don't eat with your hands!
Mmmf...
Use your fork!

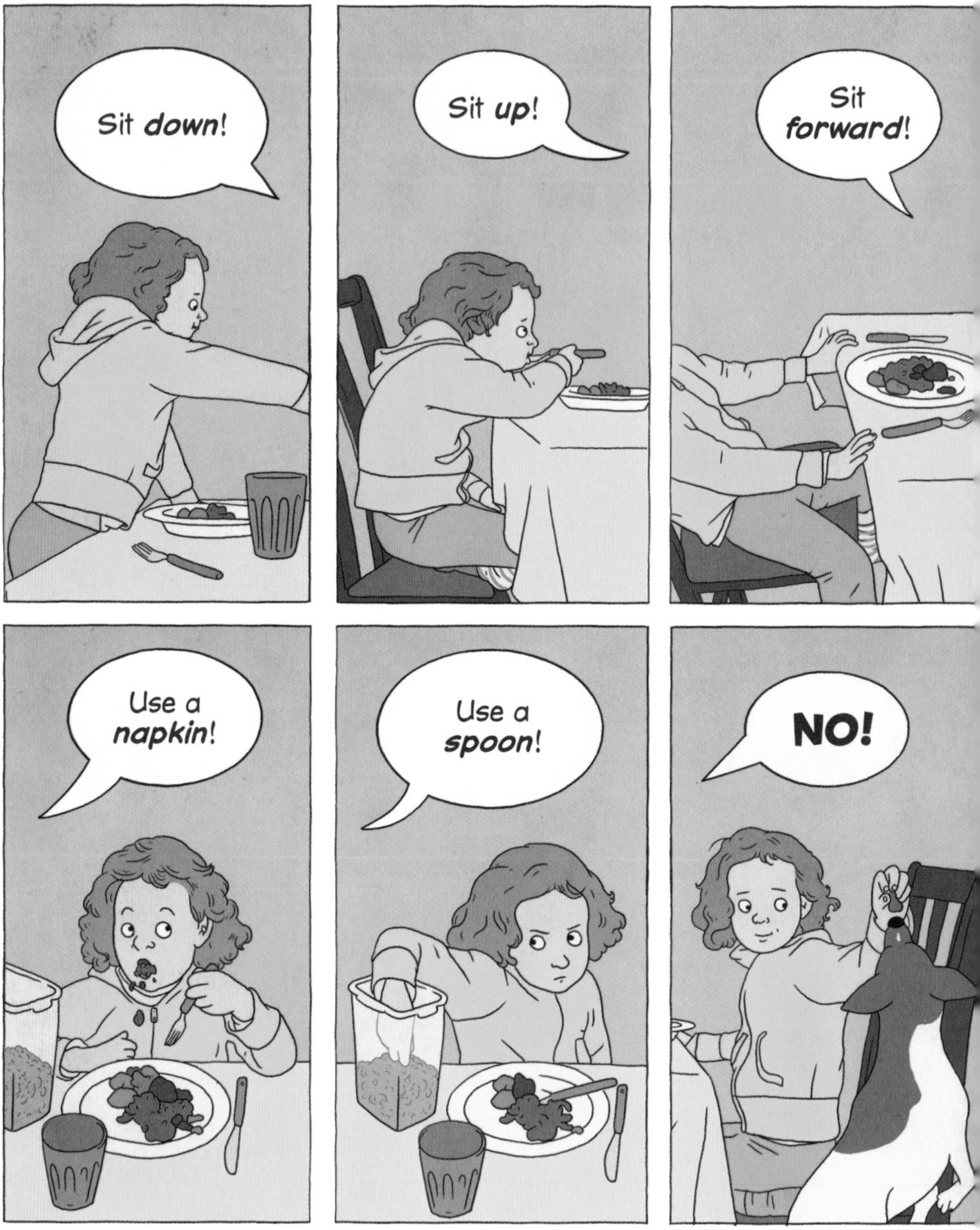
Sit *down*!
Sit *up*!
Sit *forward*!
Use a *napkin*!
Use a *spoon*!
NO!

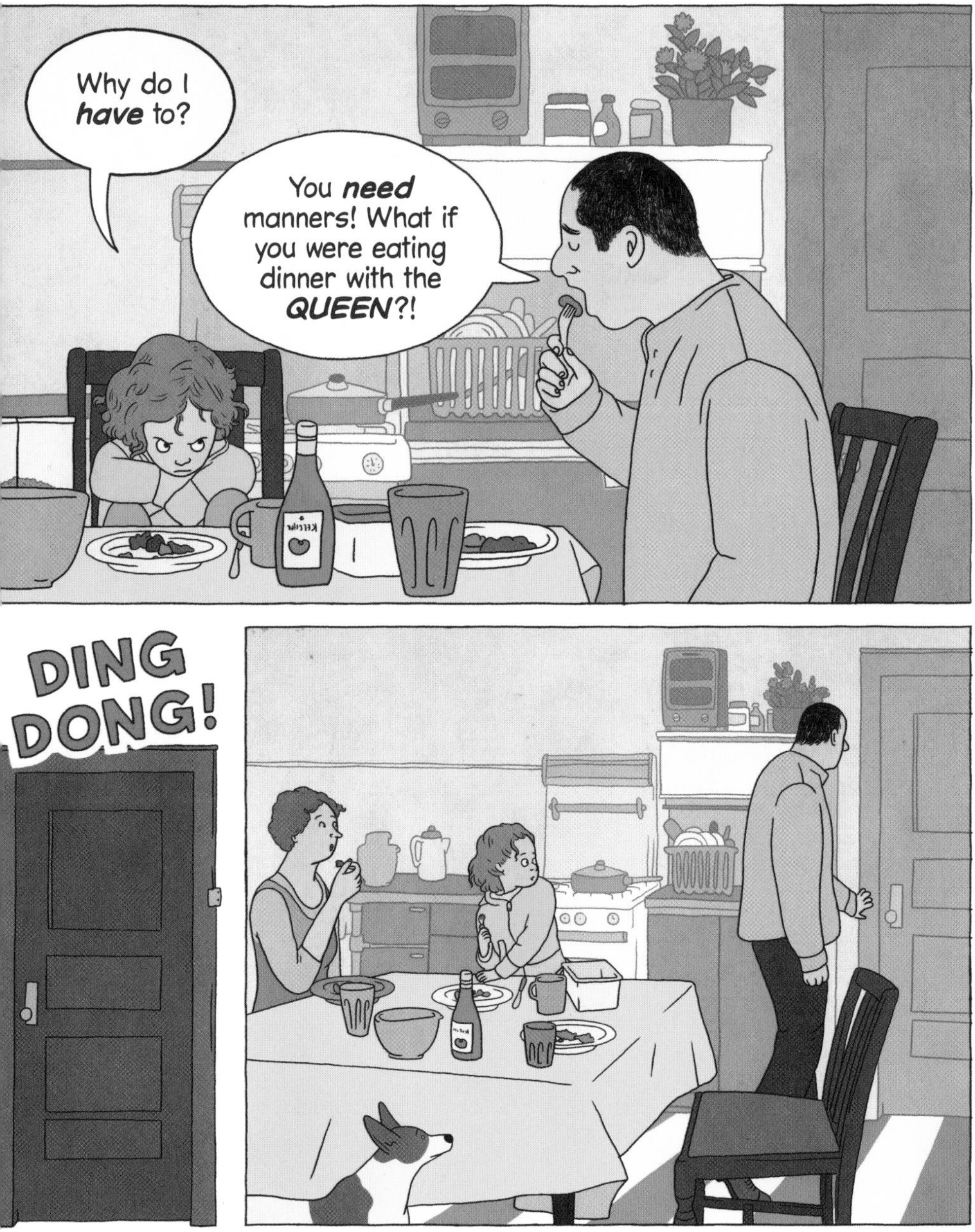
Why do I *have* to?
You *need* manners! What if you were eating dinner with the *QUEEN*?!
DING DONG!

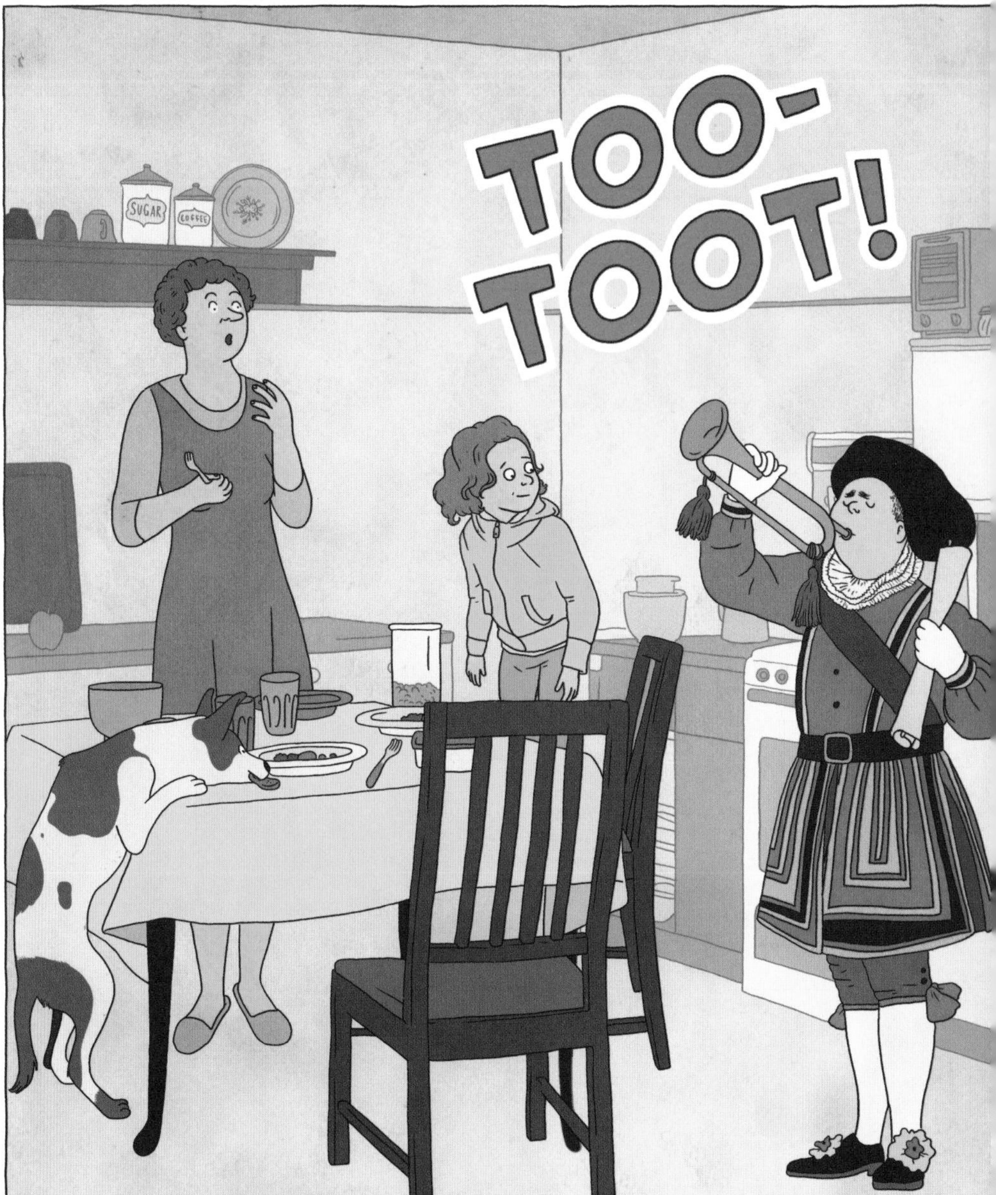
TOO-
TOOT!
SUGAR
COFFEE

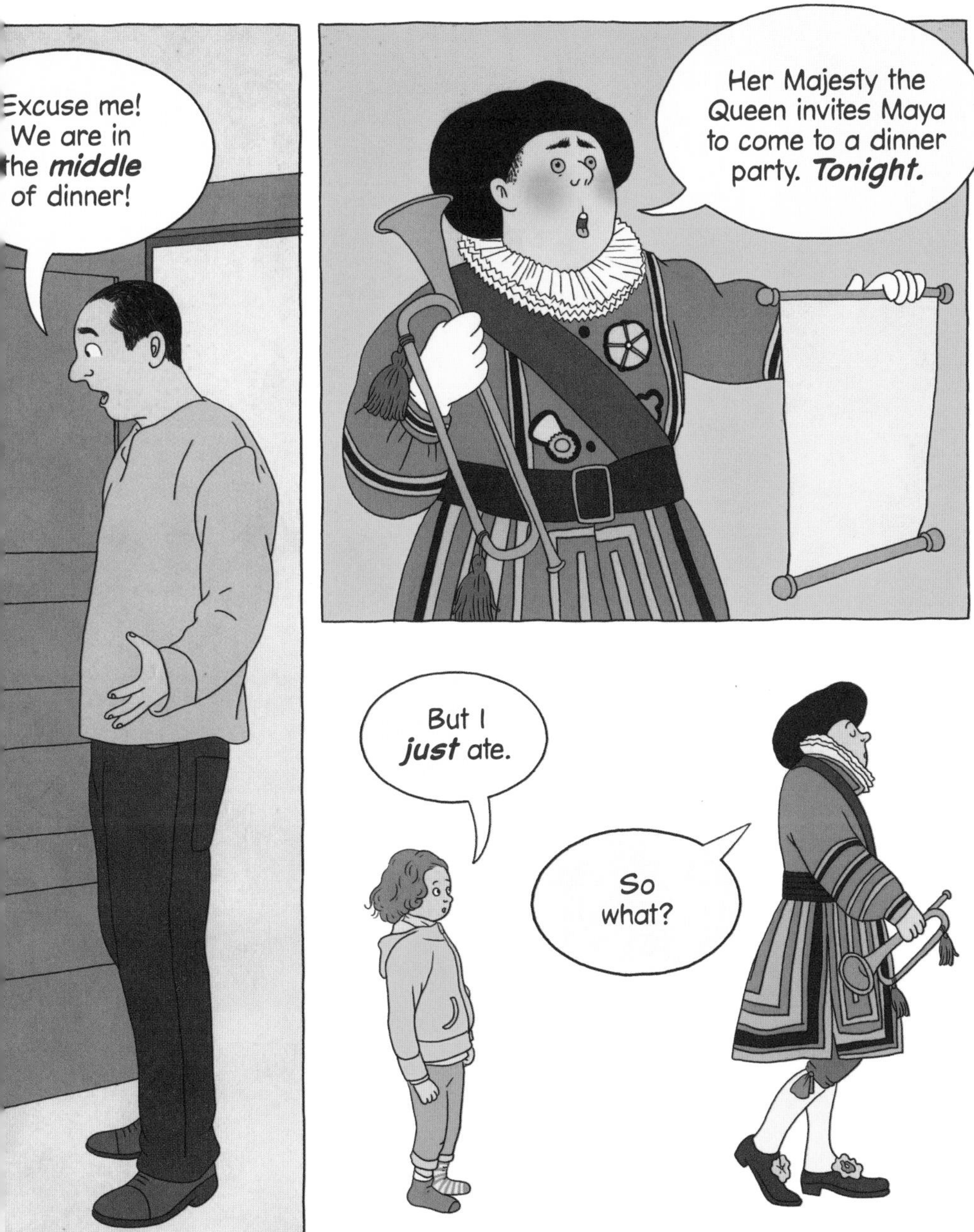
Excuse me! We are in the *middle* of dinner!
Her Majesty the Queen invites Maya to come to a dinner party. *Tonight.*
But I *just* ate.
So what?

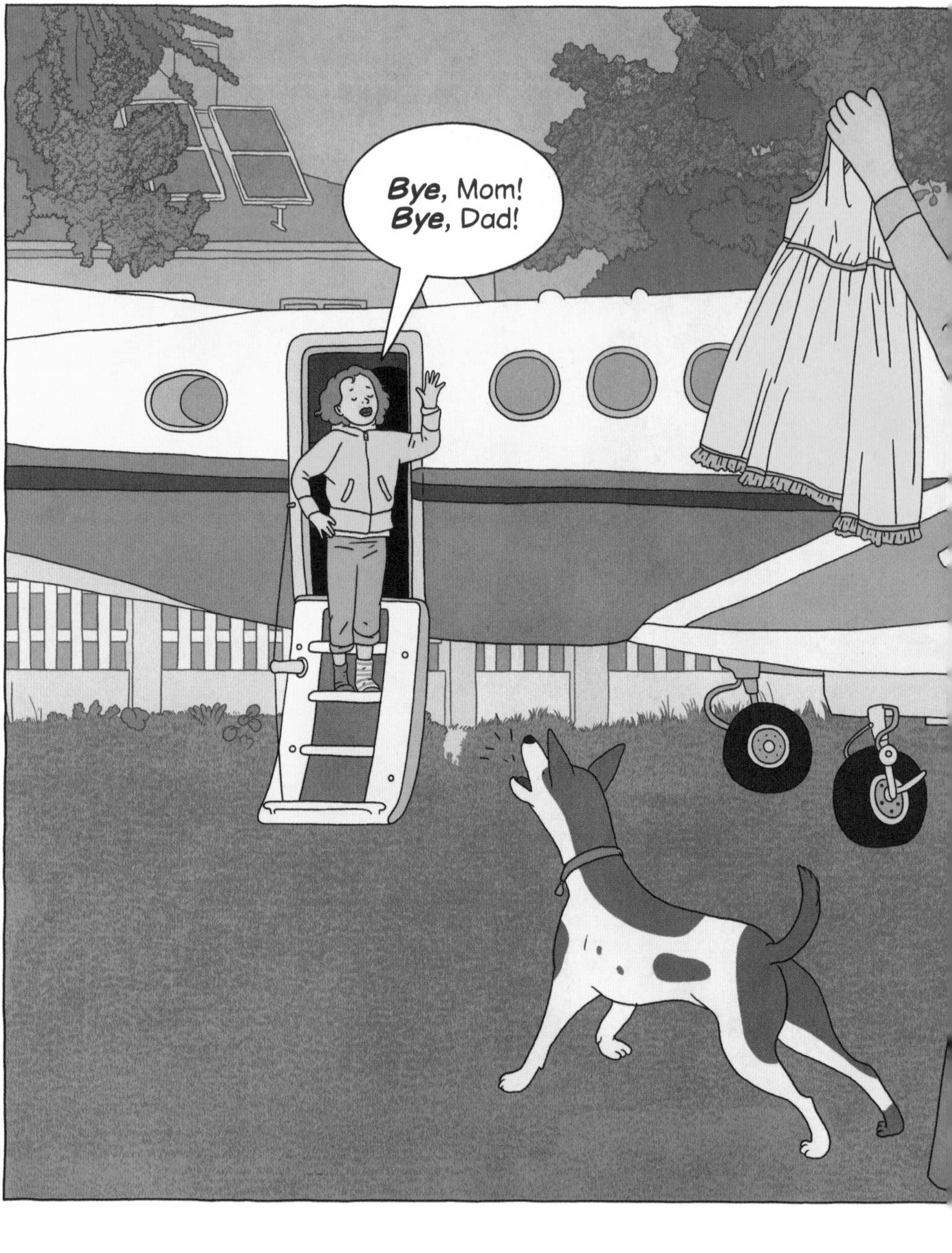
Bye, Mom!
Bye, Dad!

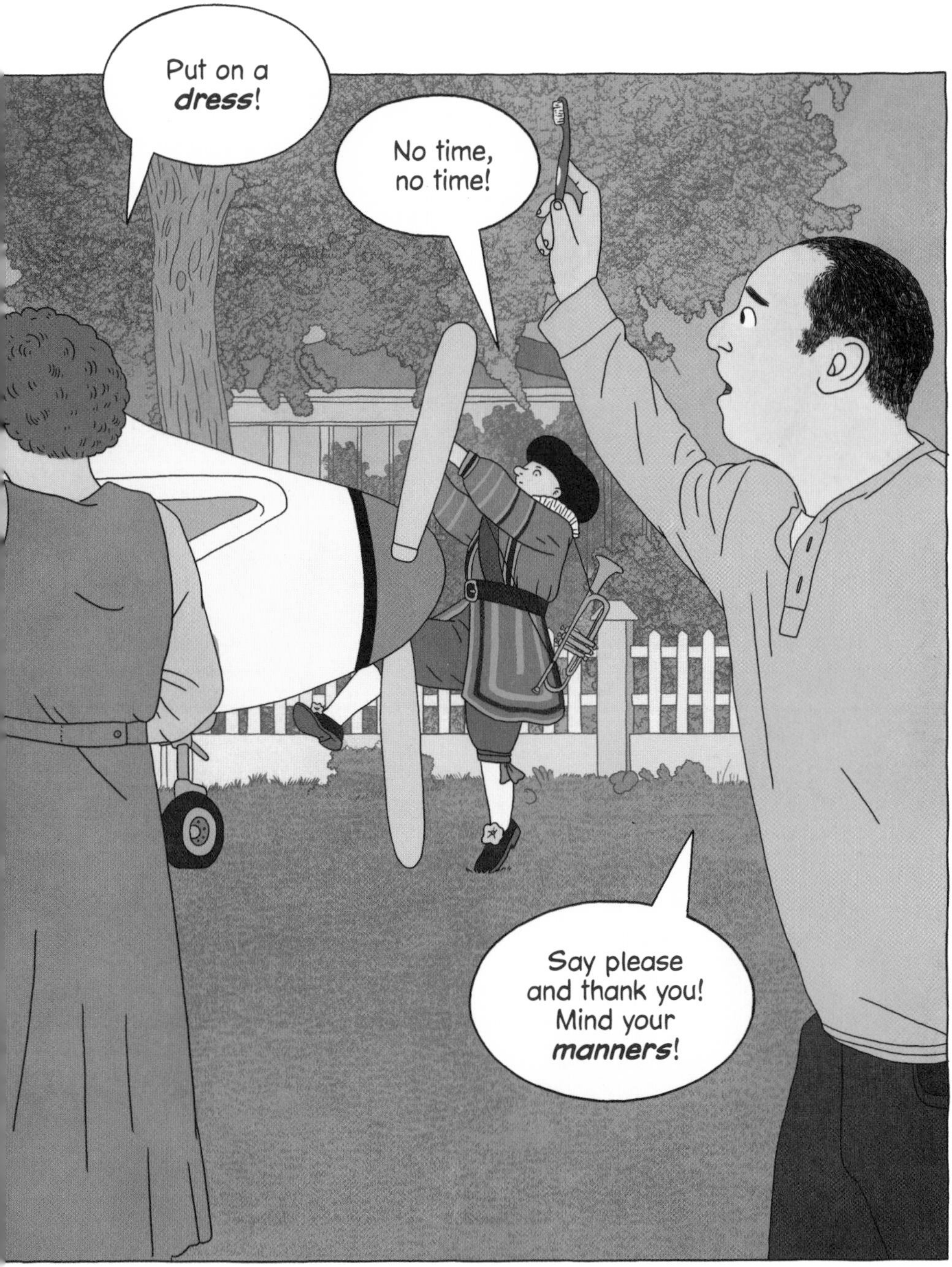
Put on a **dress**!
No time, no time!
Say please and thank you! Mind your **manners**!

Juice and cookies?
Uh...
Are you all right, honey?
I've never ***met*** a ***queen*** before..
As long as you mind your ***manners,*** the Queen will be nice.

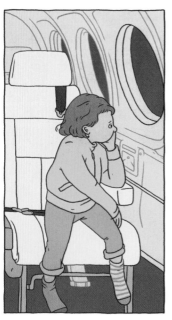

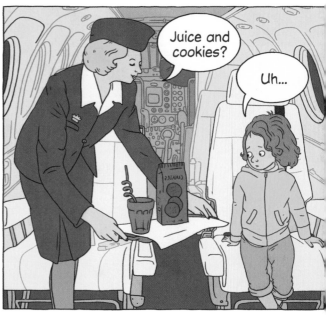

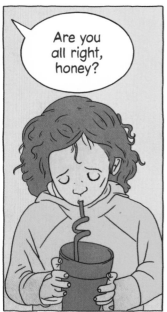

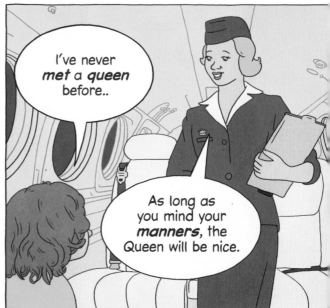

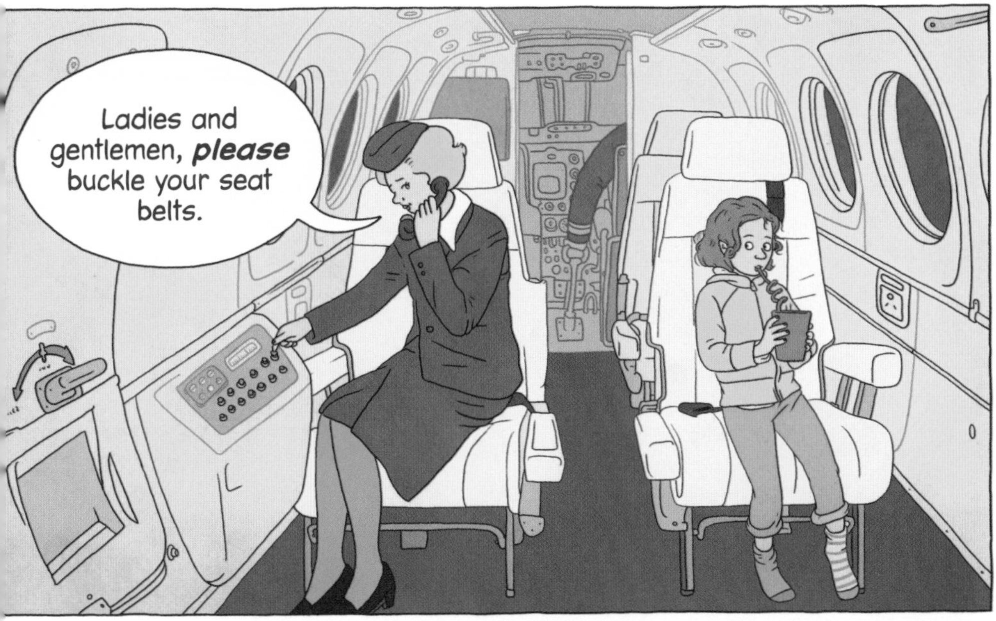
Ladies and gentlemen, ***please*** buckle your seat belts.

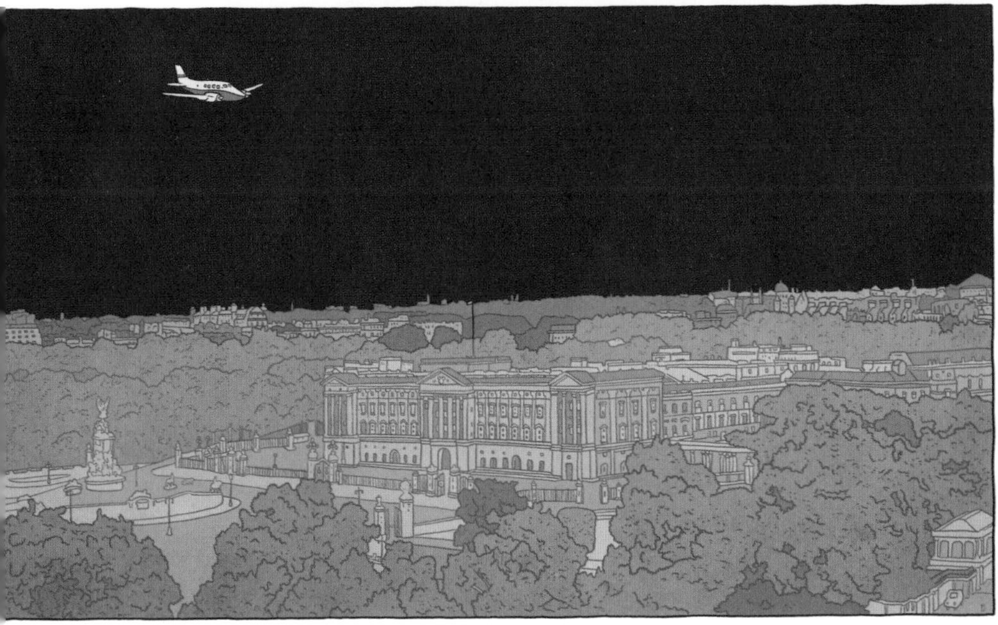

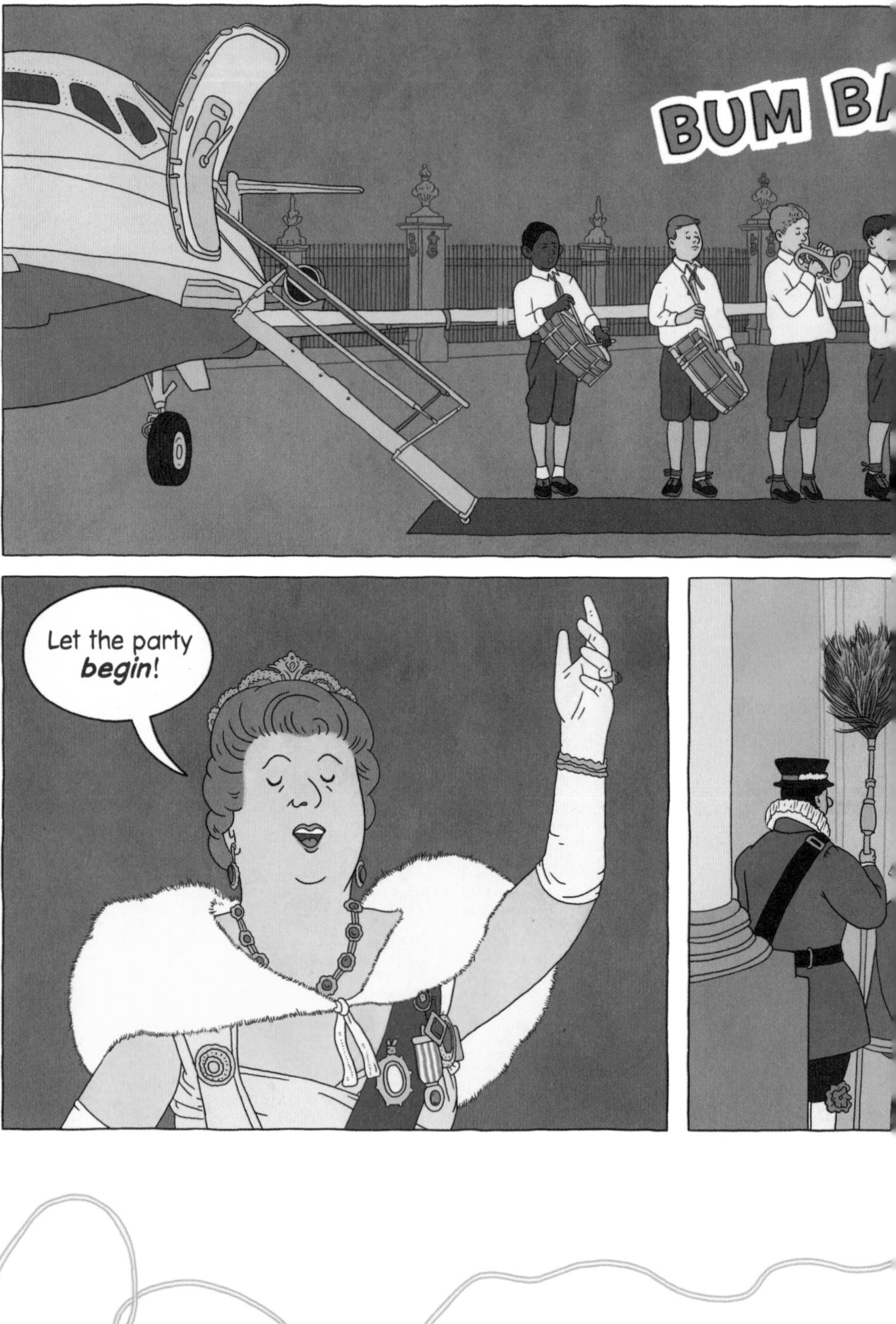
BUM B
Let the party *begin*!

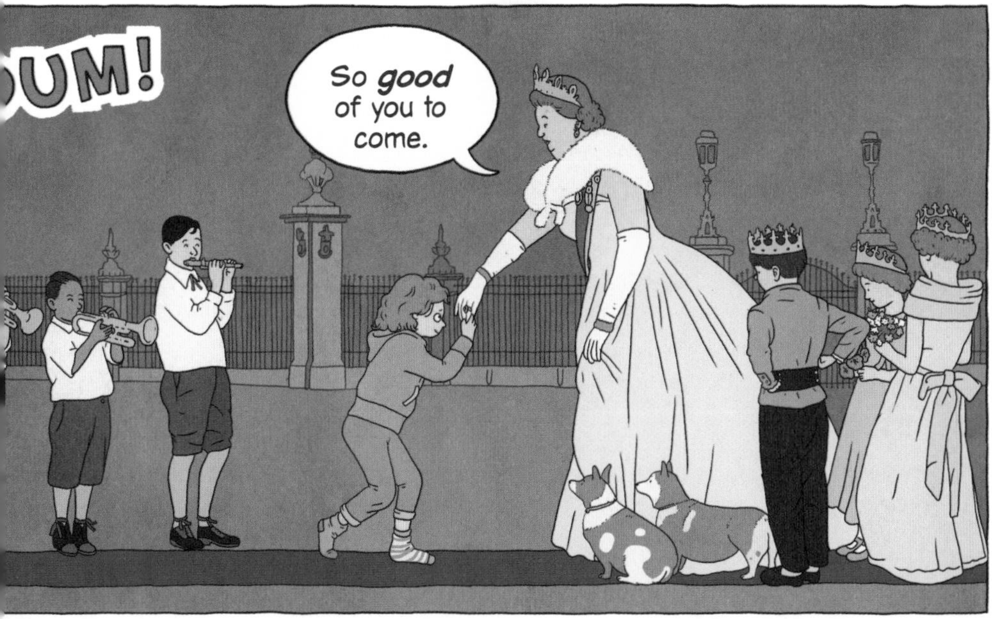
UM!
So *good* of you to come.

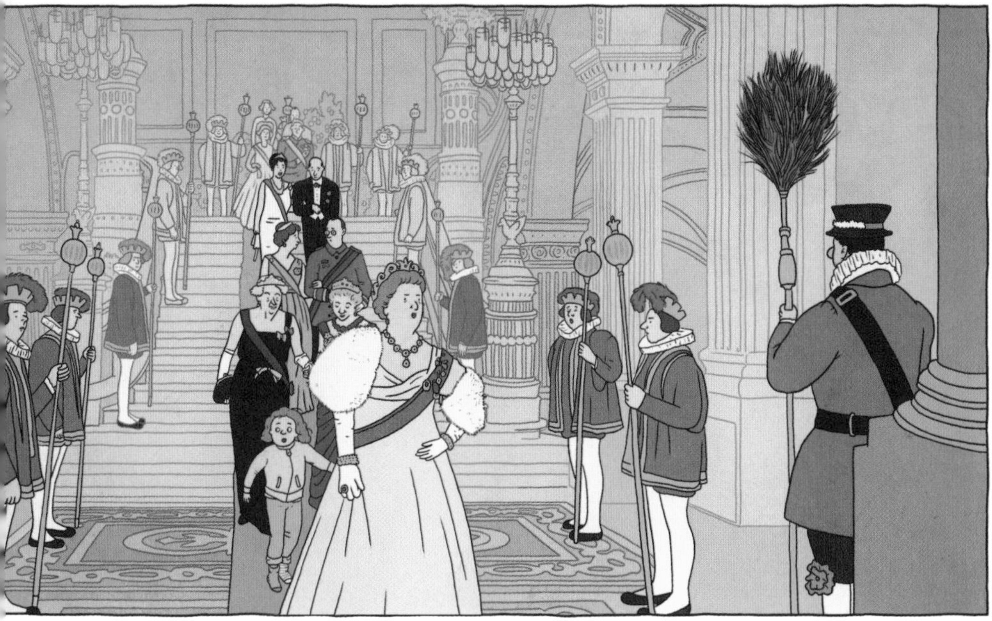

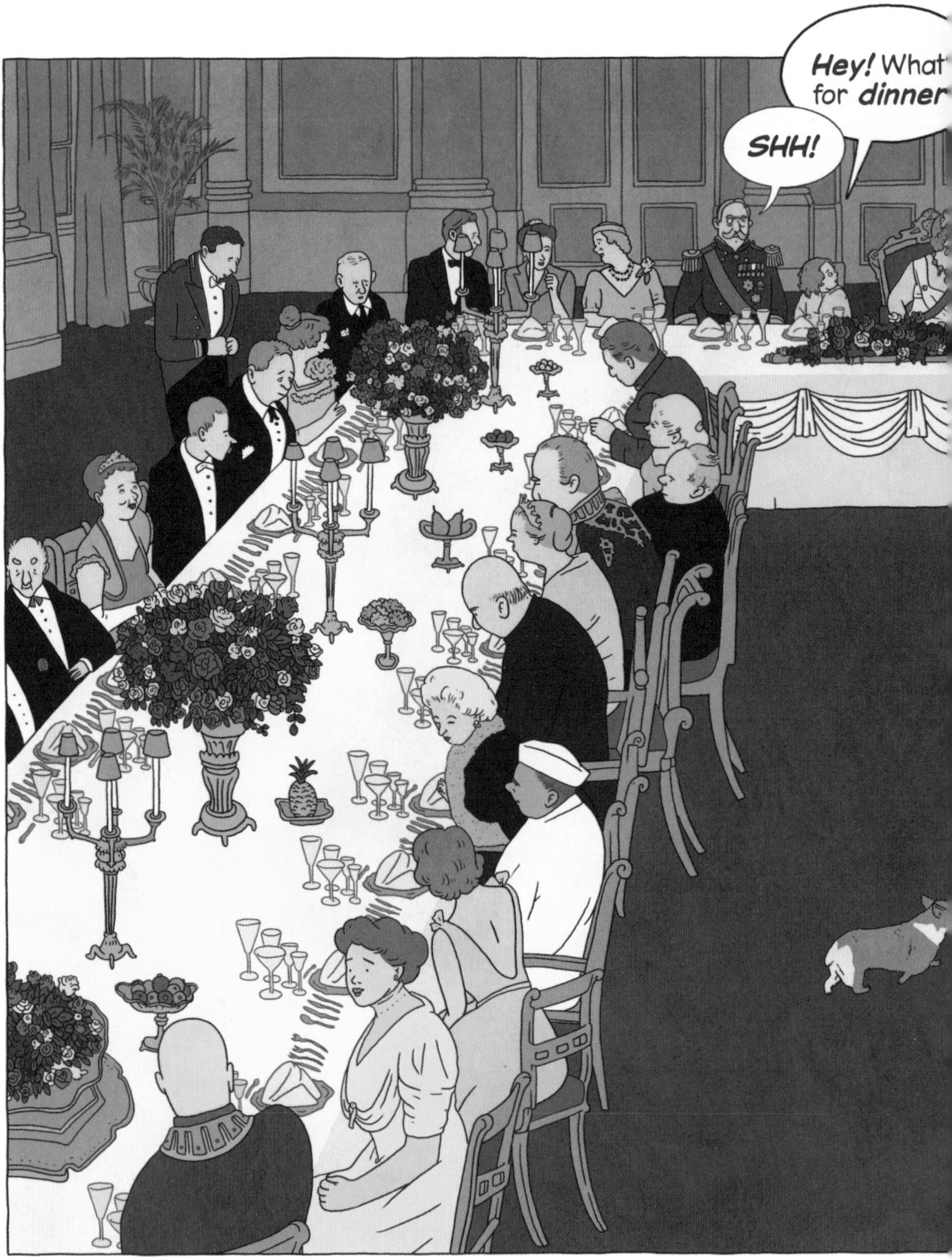
Hey! What
for dinner
SHH!

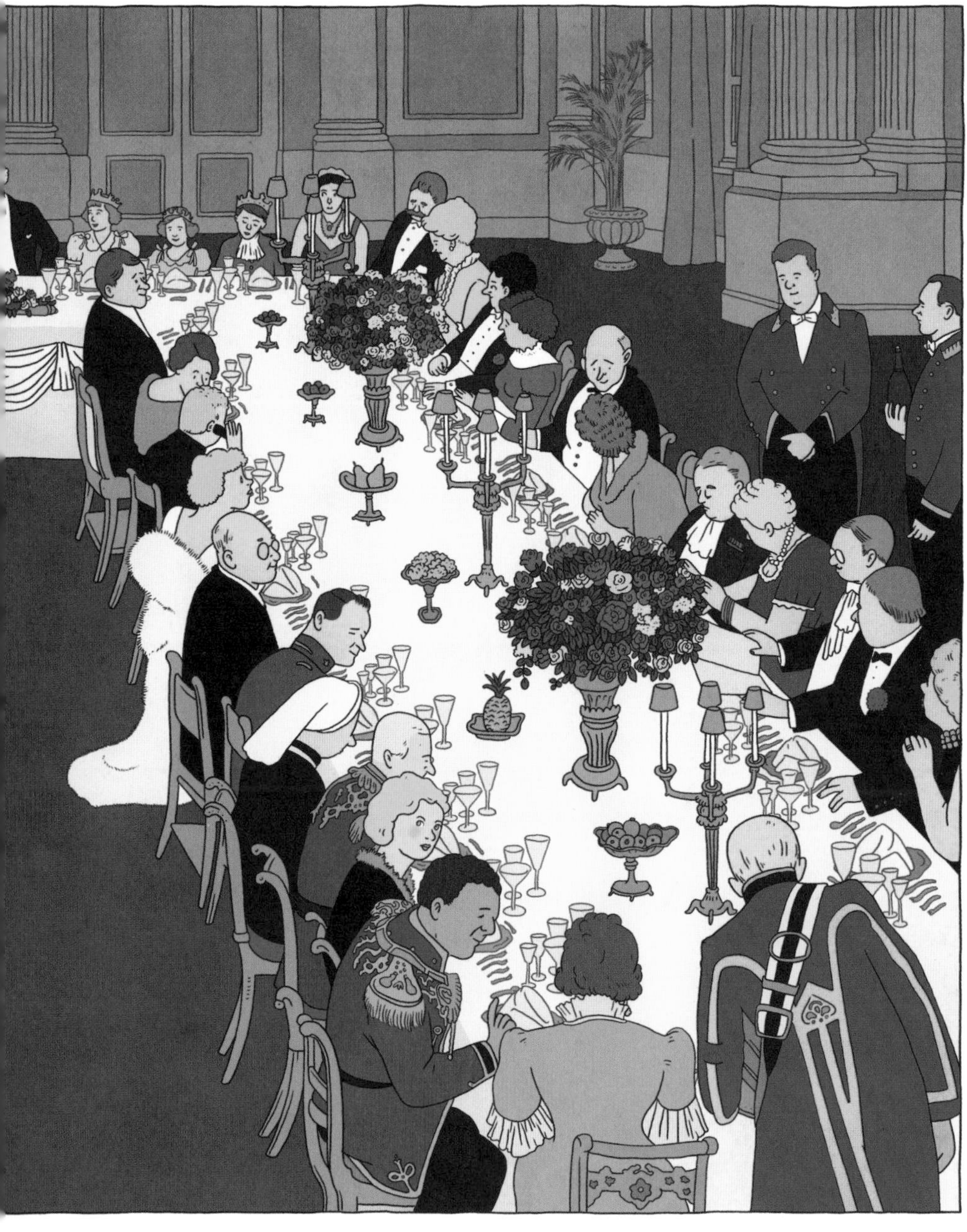

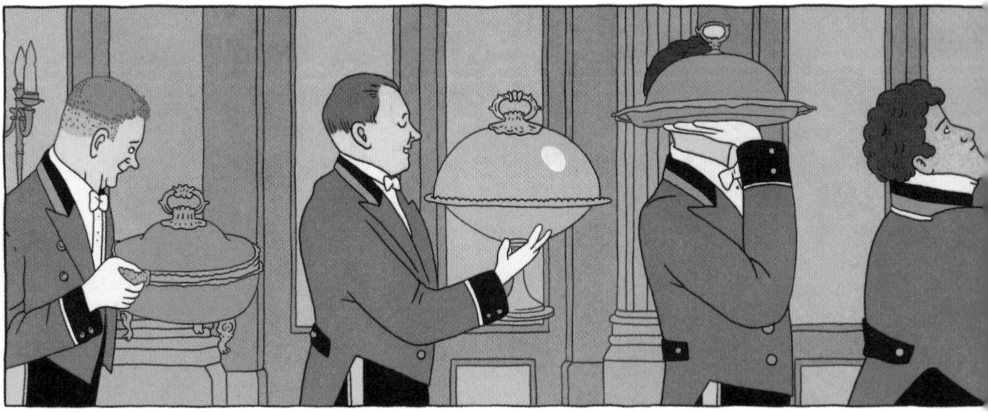

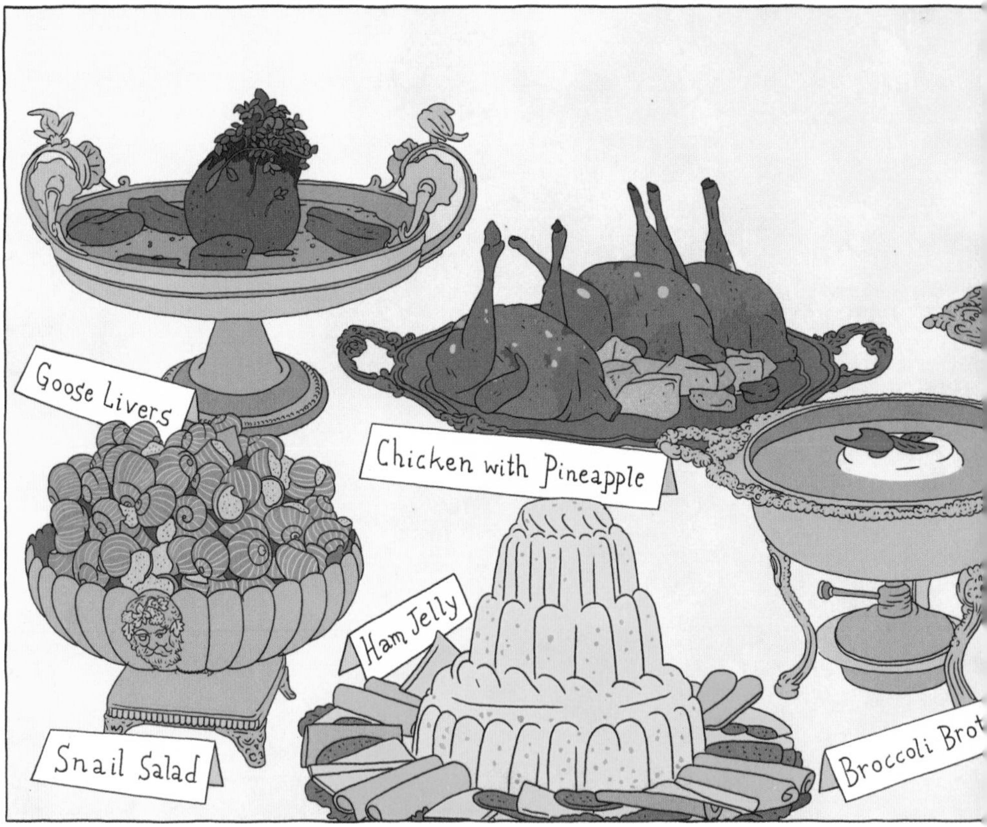
Goose Livers
Chicken with Pineapple
Ham Jelly
Snail Salad
Broccoli Brot

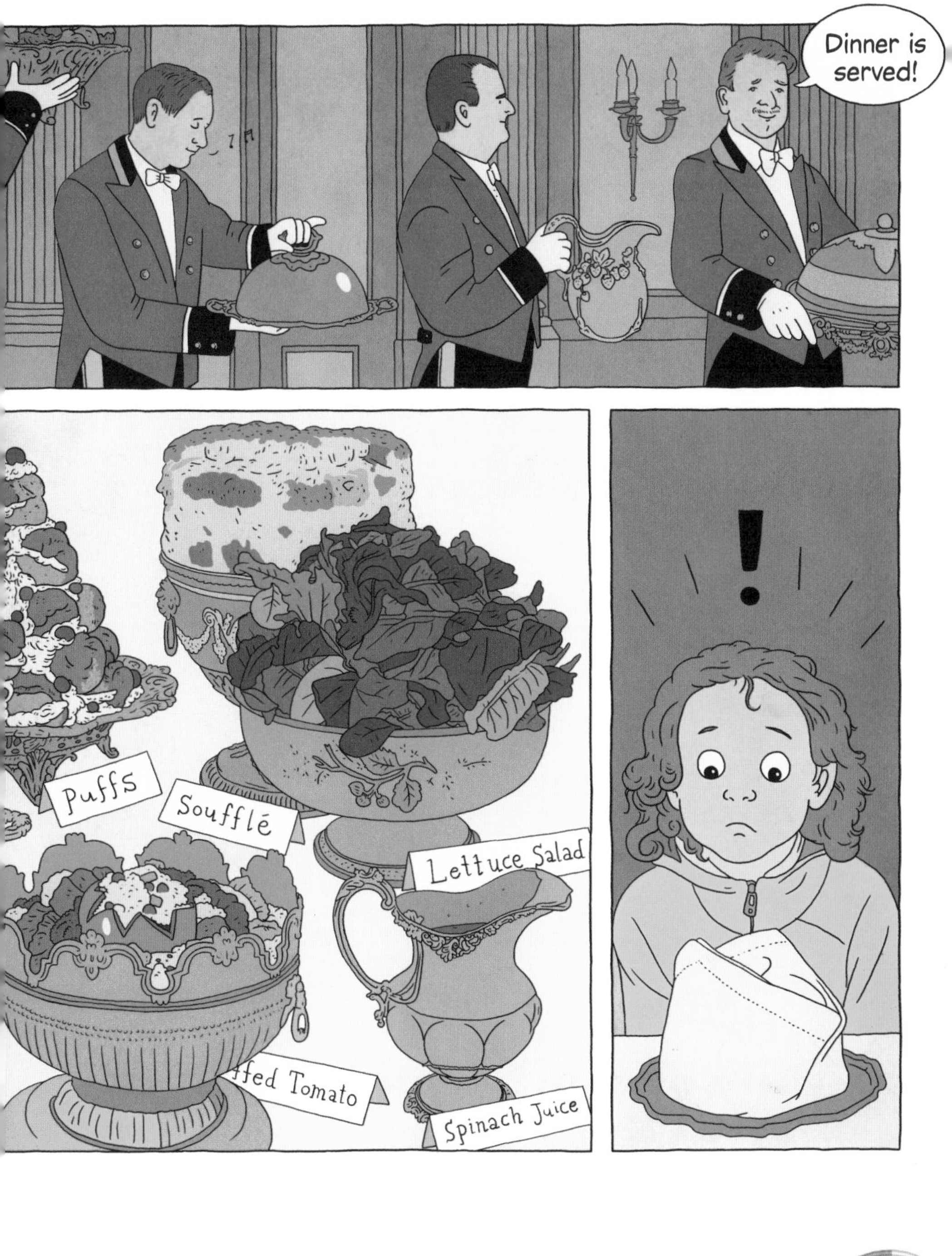
Dinner is served!
Puffs
Soufflé
Lettuce Salad
ffed Tomato
Spinach Juice
!

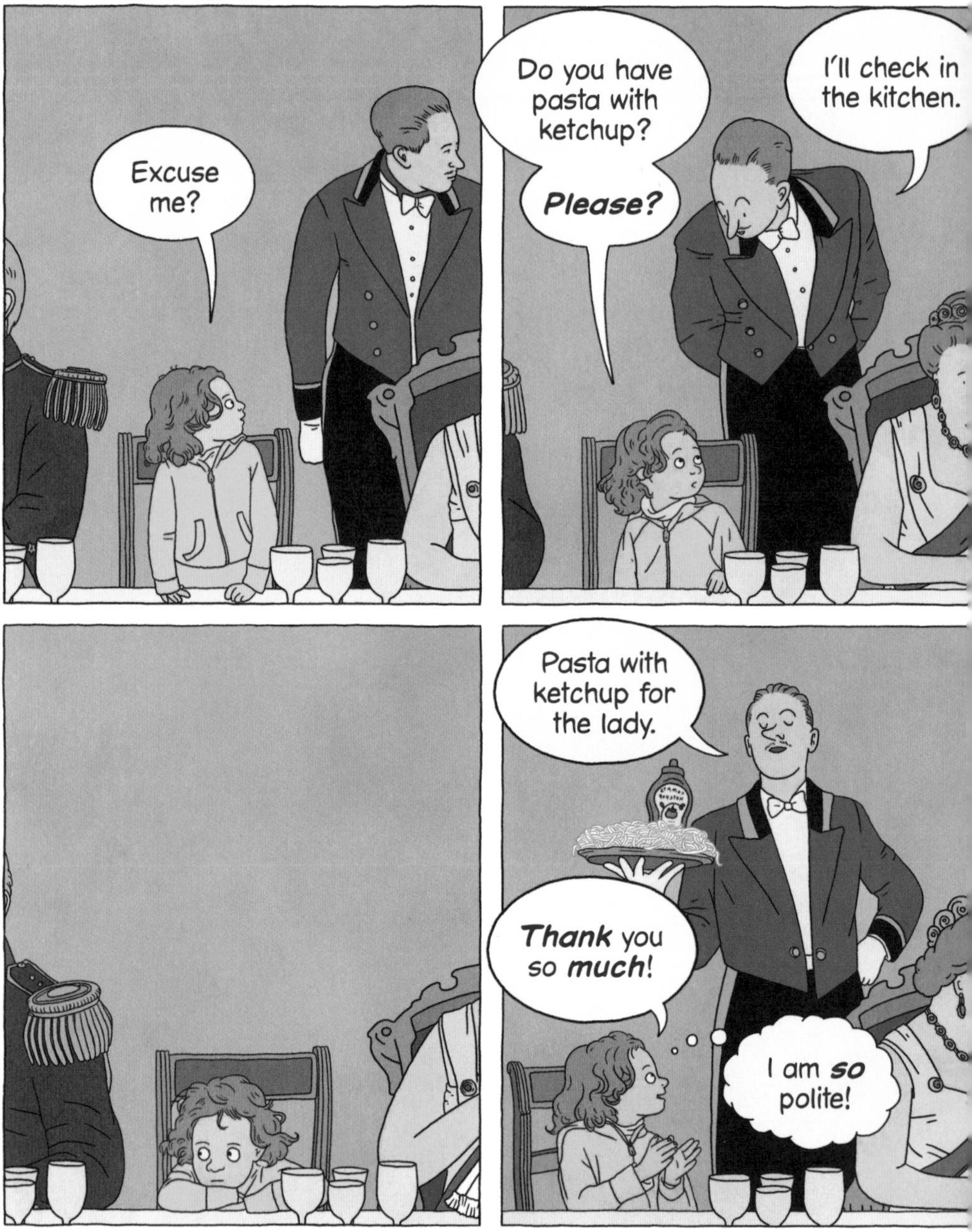
Excuse me?
Do you have pasta with ketchup?
Please?
I'll check in the kitchen.
Pasta with ketchup for the lady.
Thank you so much!
I am so polite!

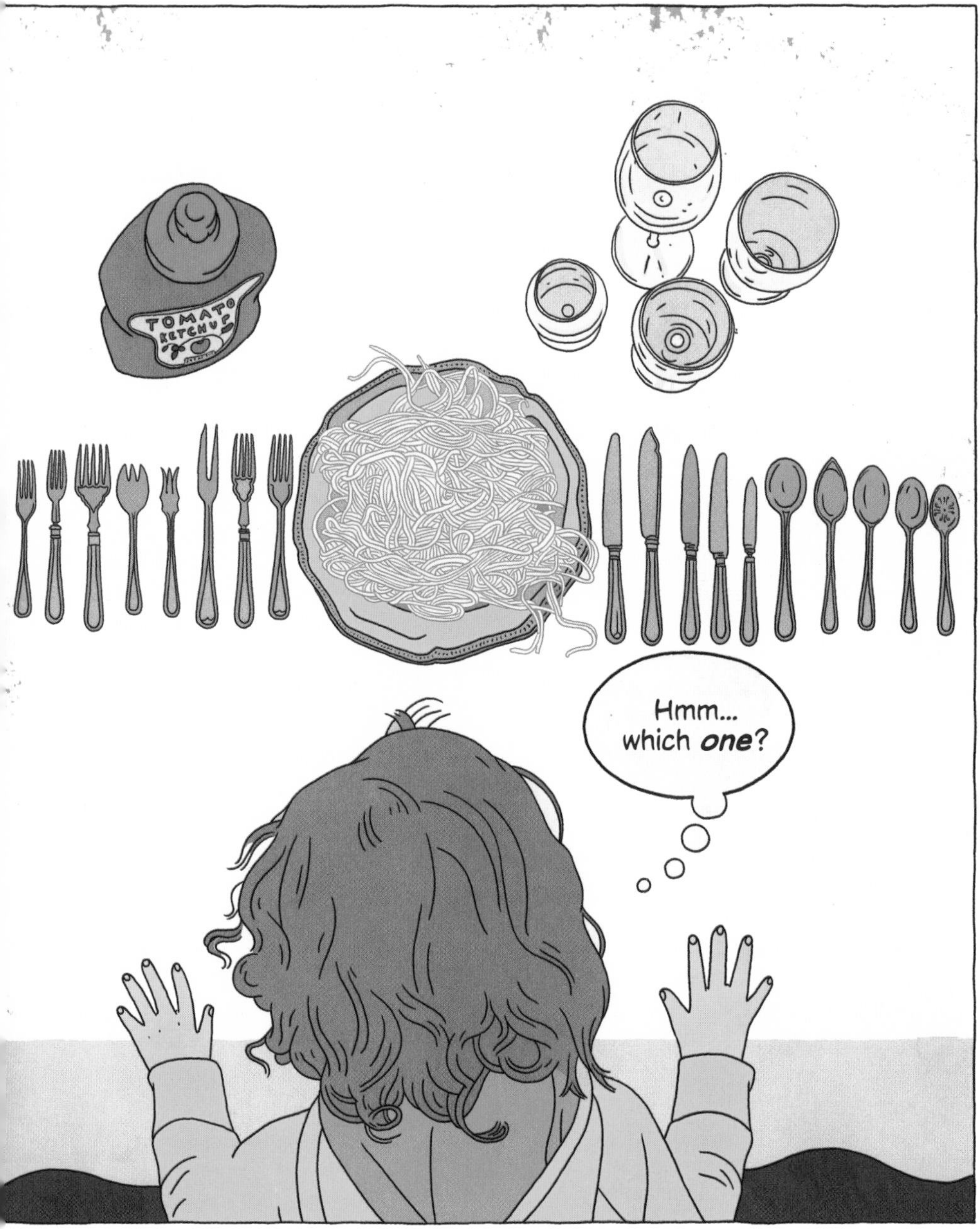
TOMATO KETCHUP
Hmm... which *one*?

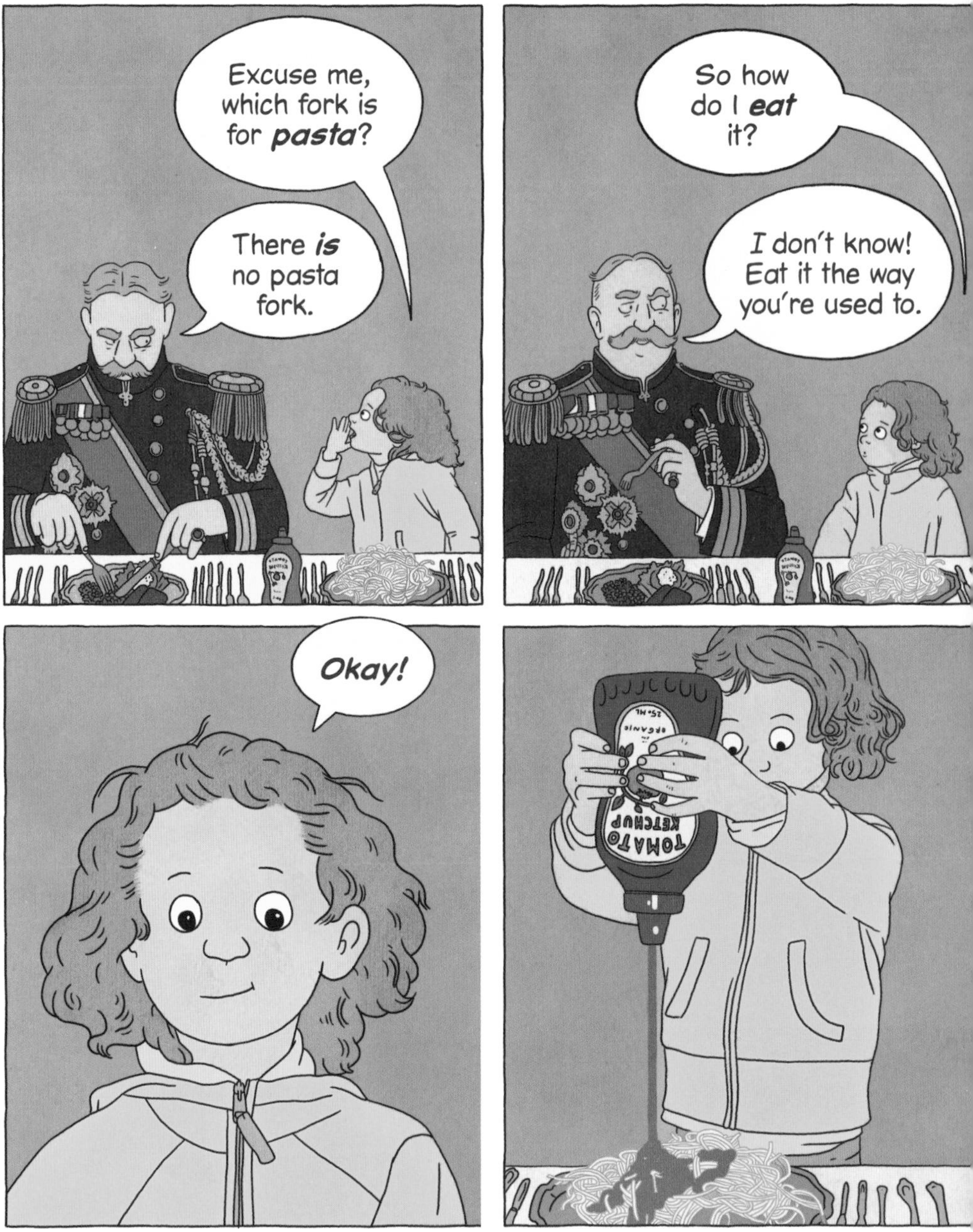
Excuse me, which fork is for *pasta*?
There *is* no pasta fork.
So how do I *eat* it?
I don't know! Eat it the way you're used to.
Okay!
TOMATO KETCHUP

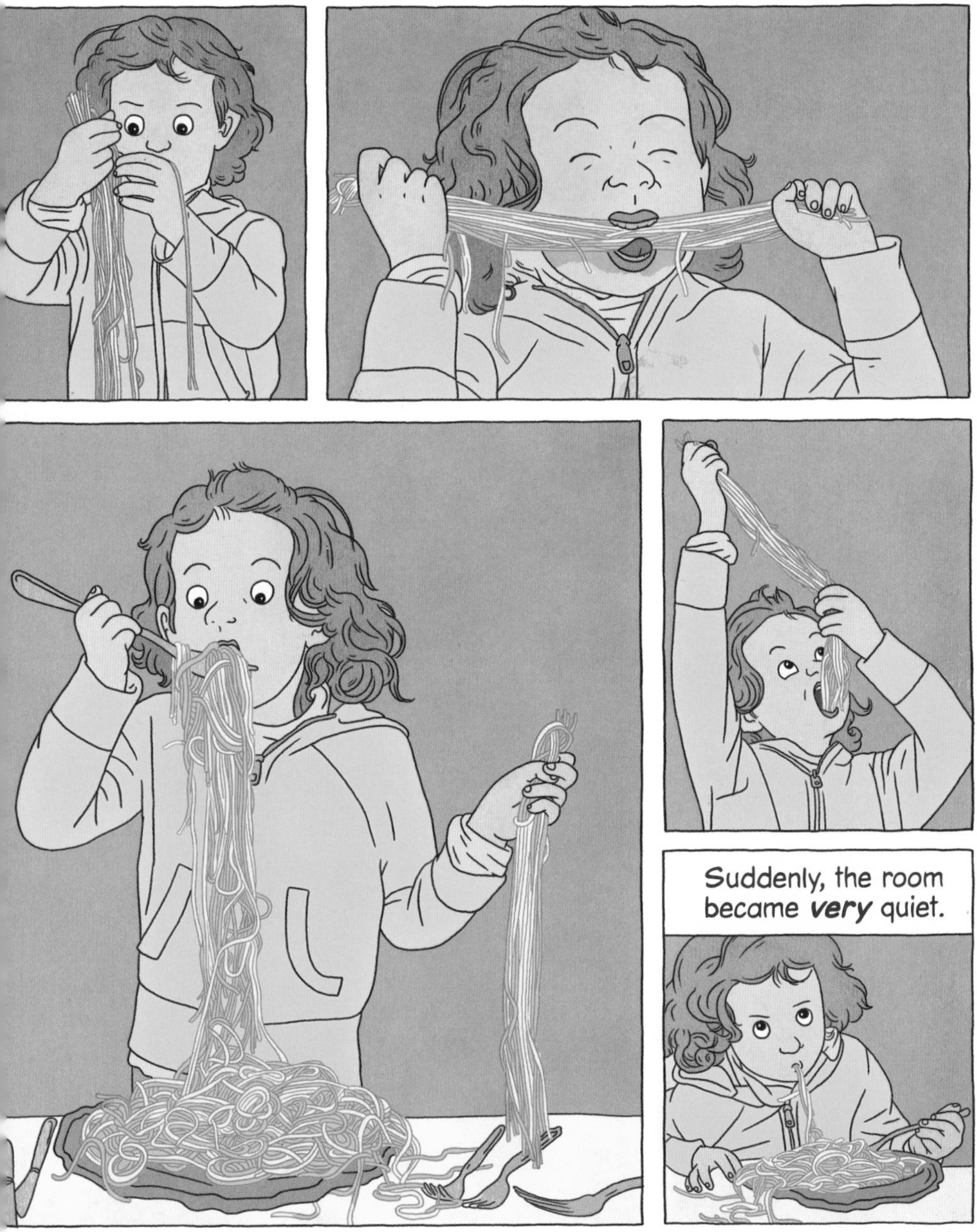
Suddenly, the room
became ***very*** quiet.

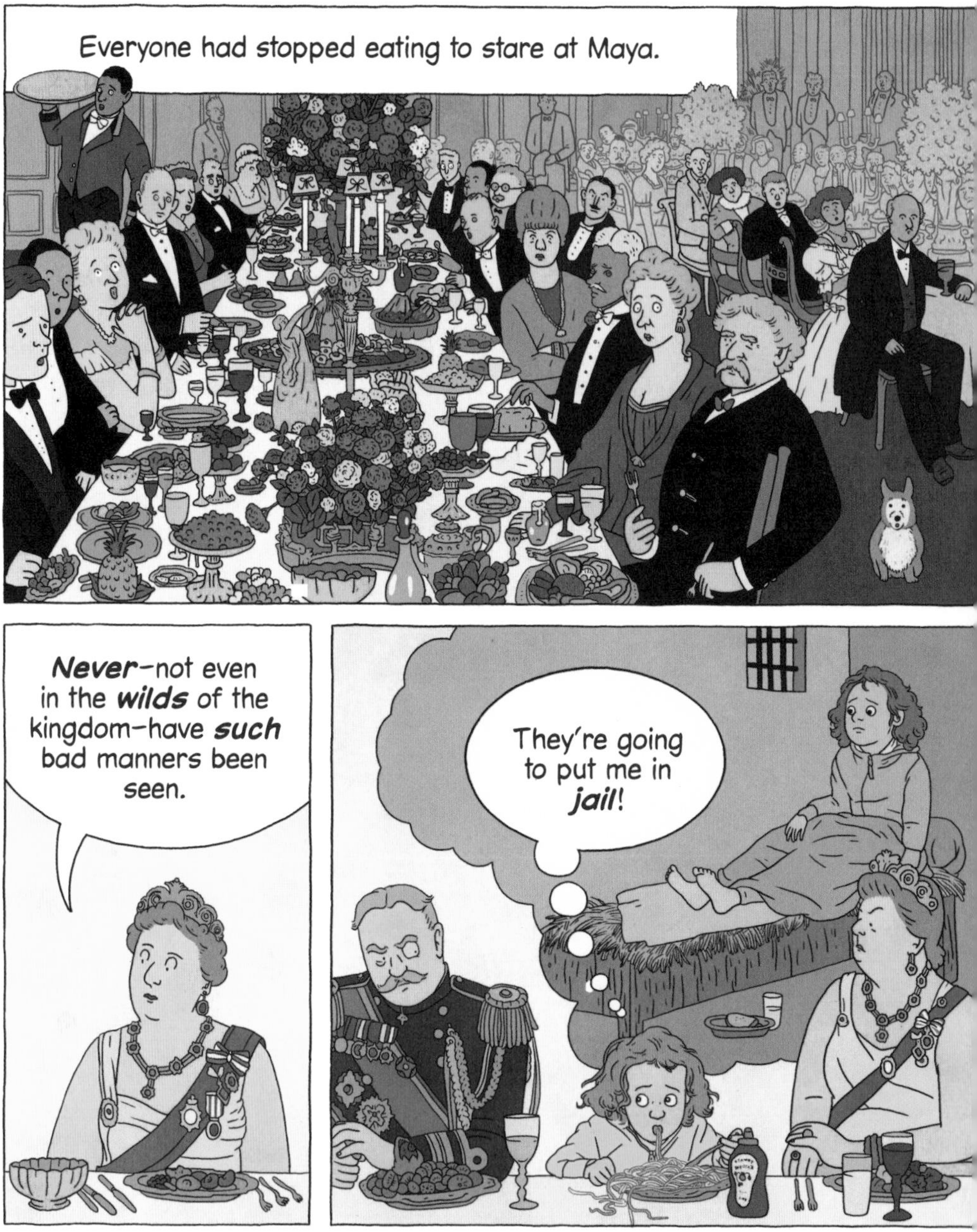
Everyone had stopped eating to stare at Maya.
Never—not even in the wilds of the kingdom—have such bad manners been seen.
They're going to put me in jail!

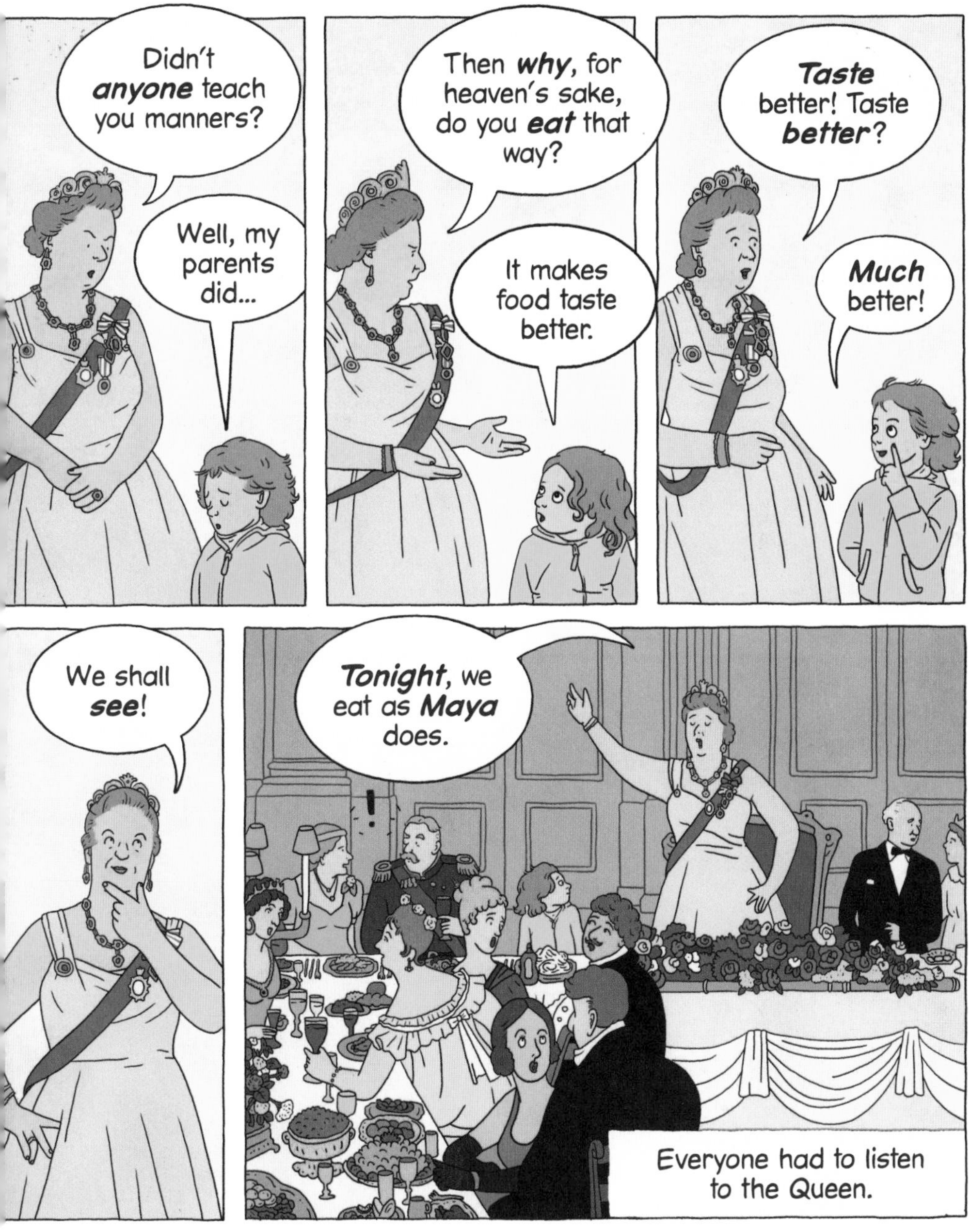
Didn't **anyone** teach you manners?
Well, my parents did...
Then **why**, for heaven's sake, do you **eat** that way?
It makes food taste better.
Taste better! Taste **better**?
Much better!
We shall **see**!
Tonight, we eat as **Maya** does.
Everyone had to listen to the Queen.

The Duke ate the chicken with his hands.
The Princess put her face in the soup bowl.
The Countess put her hands in the salad.
The Duchess fed cheese to the dog.

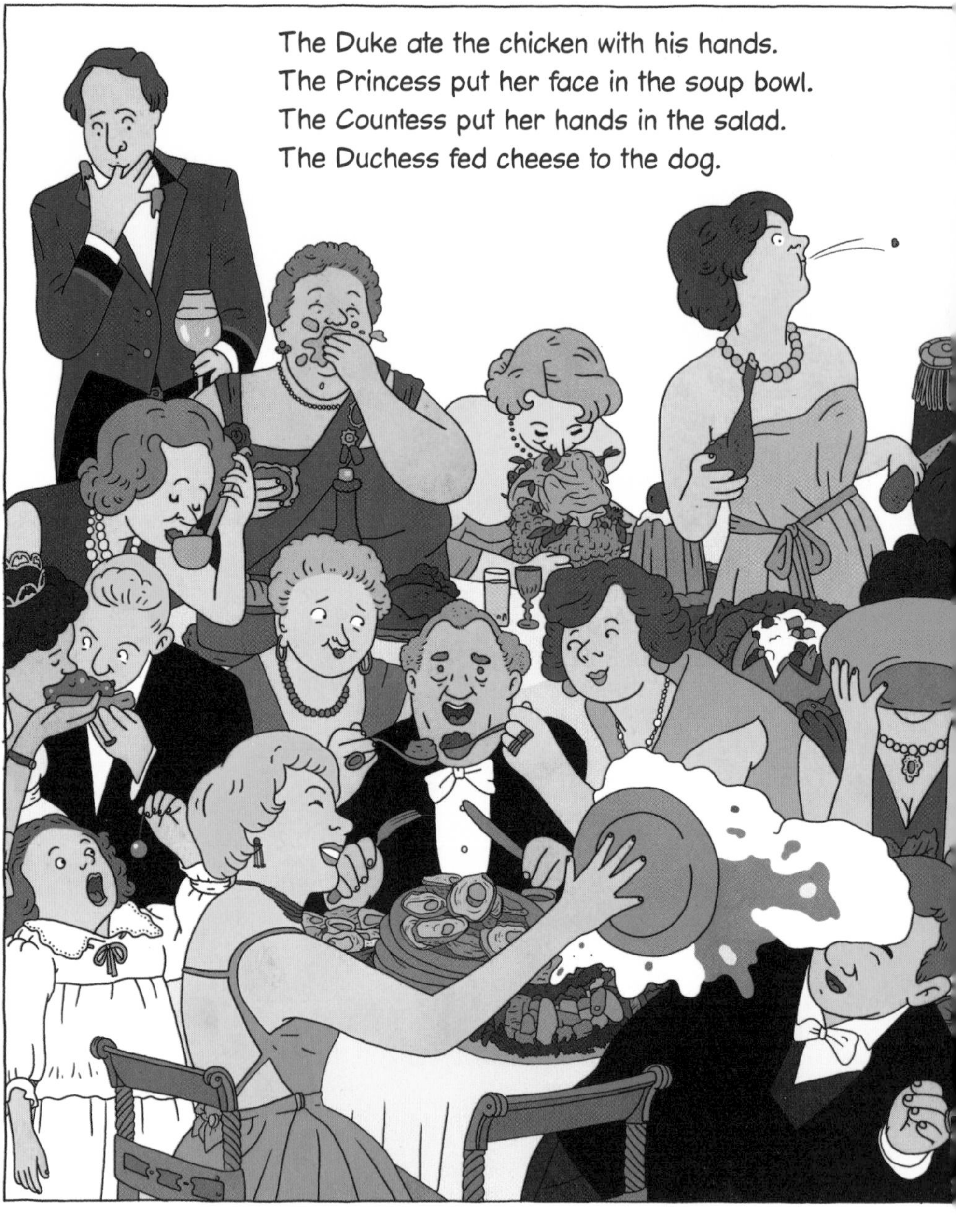

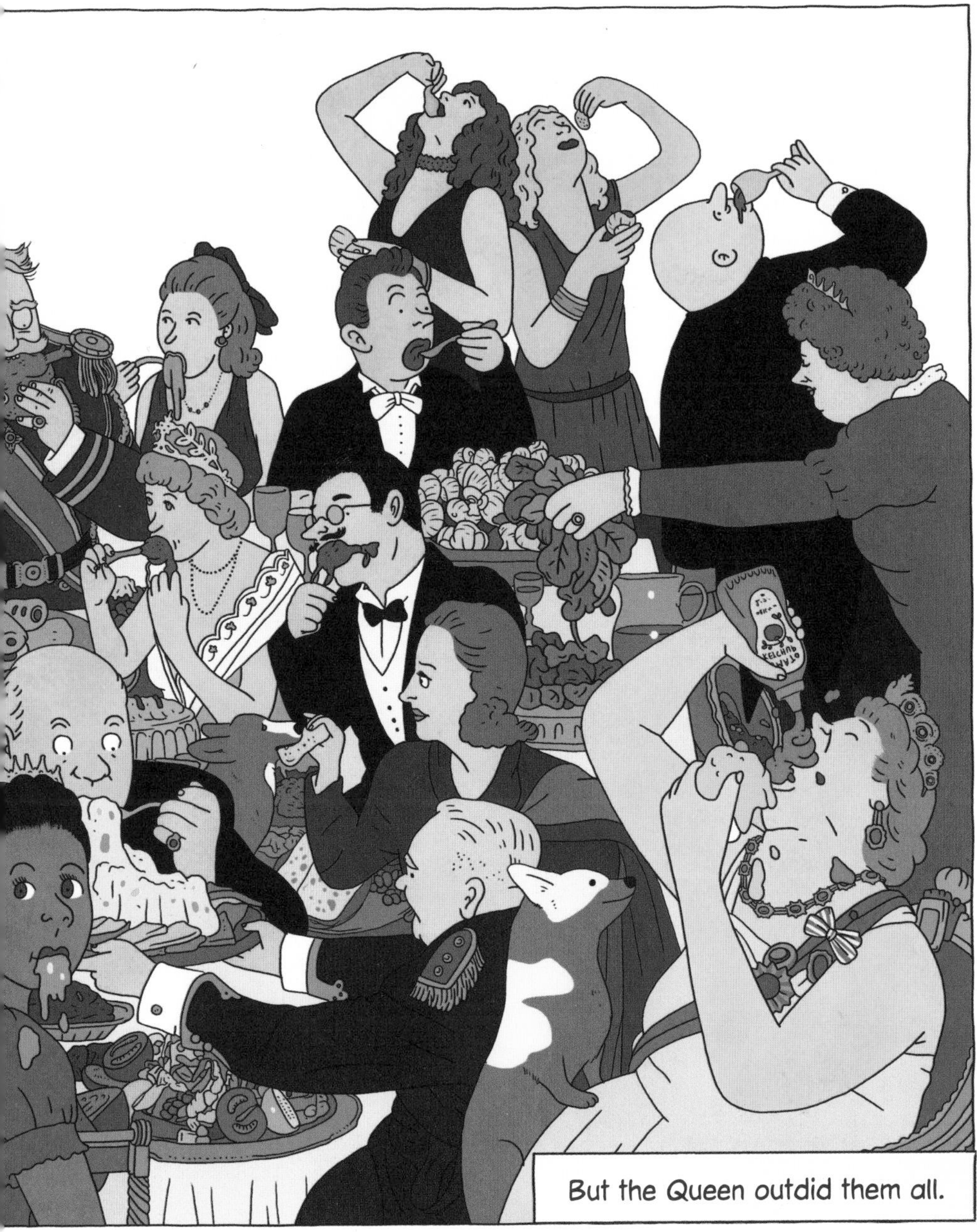
But the Queen outdid them all.

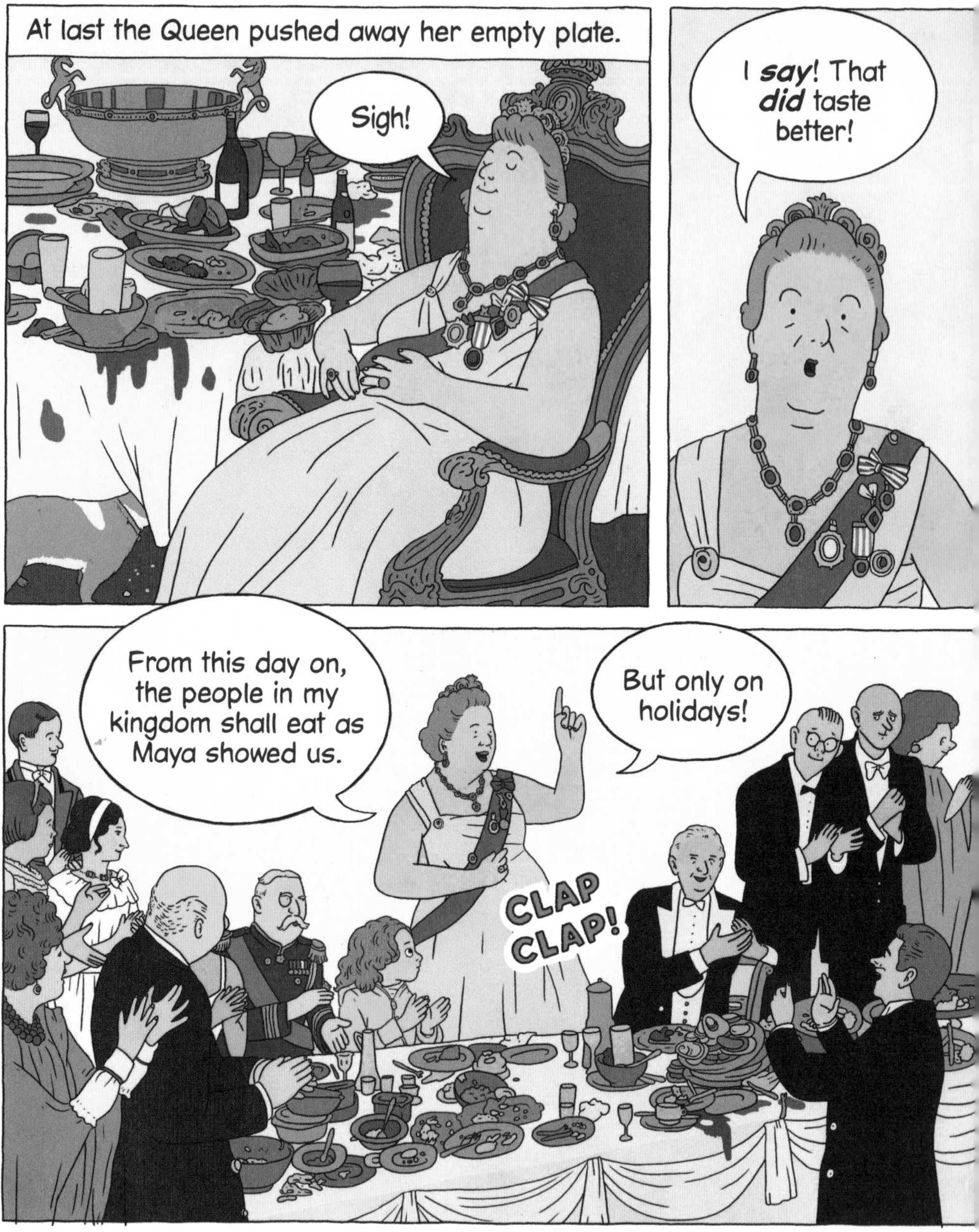
At last the Queen pushed away her empty plate.
Sigh!
I *say*! That *did* taste better!
From this day on, the people in my kingdom shall eat as Maya showed us.
But only on holidays!
CLAP CLAP!

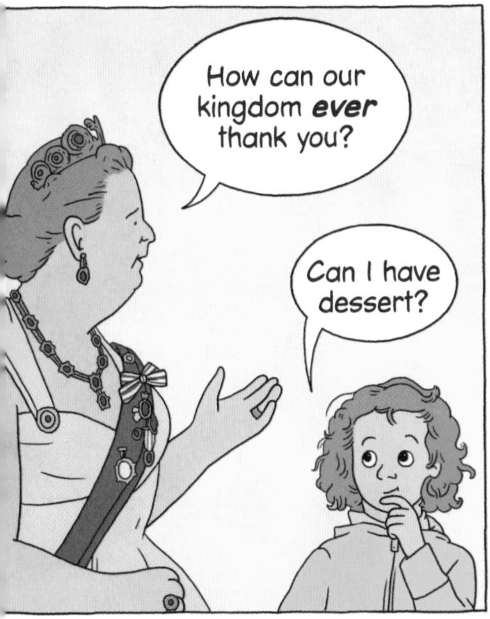
How can our kingdom **ever** thank you?
Can I have dessert?

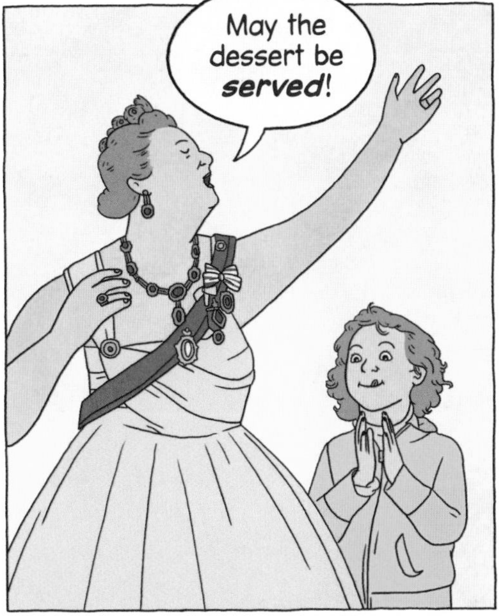
May the dessert be **served**!

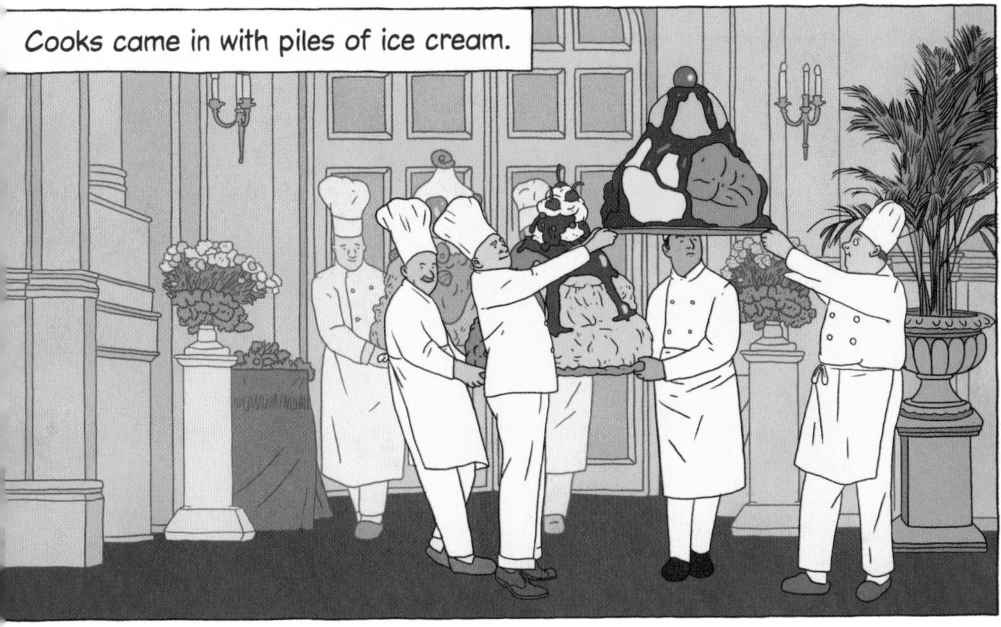
Cooks came in with piles of ice cream.

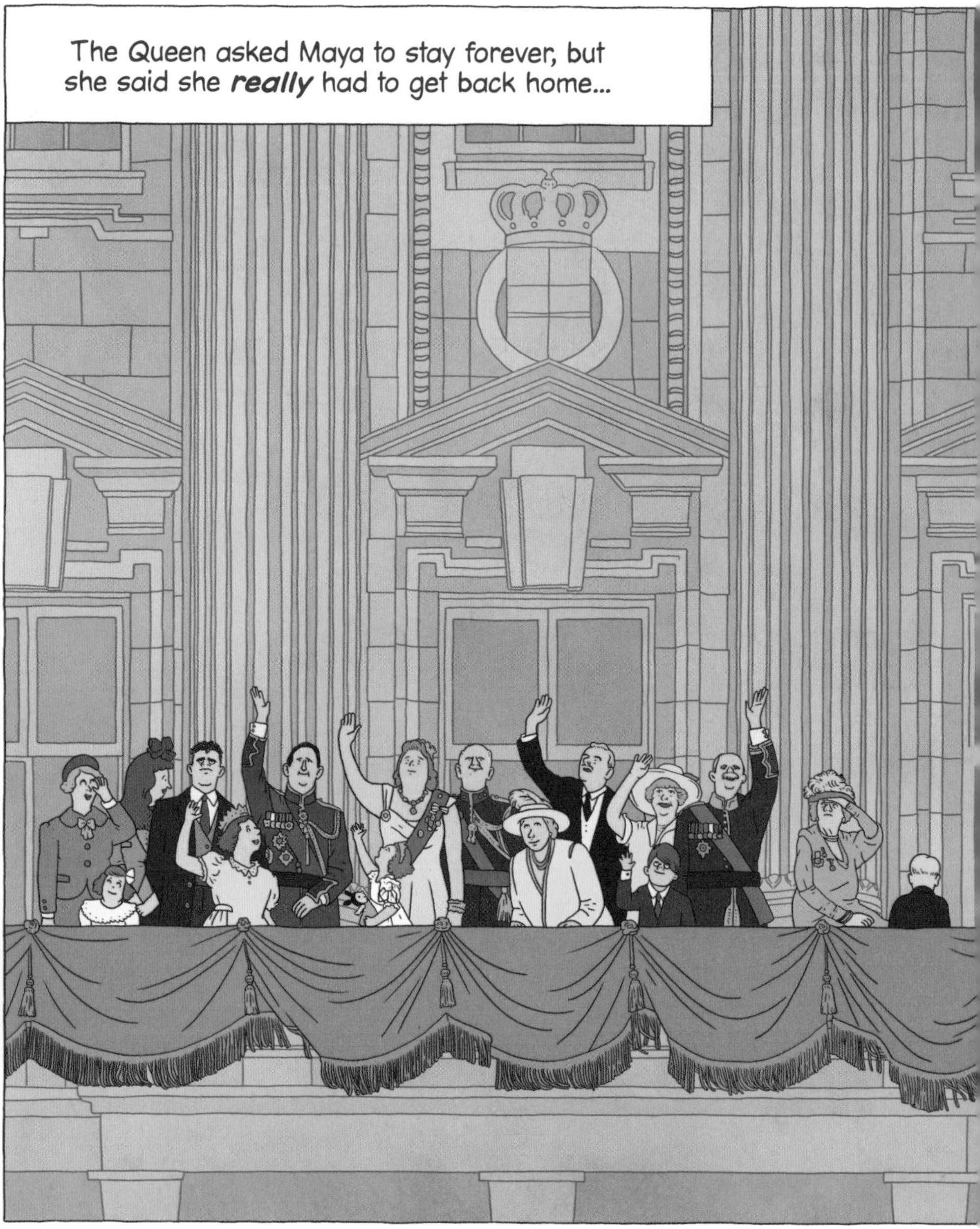
The Queen asked Maya to stay forever, but she said she ***really*** had to get back home...

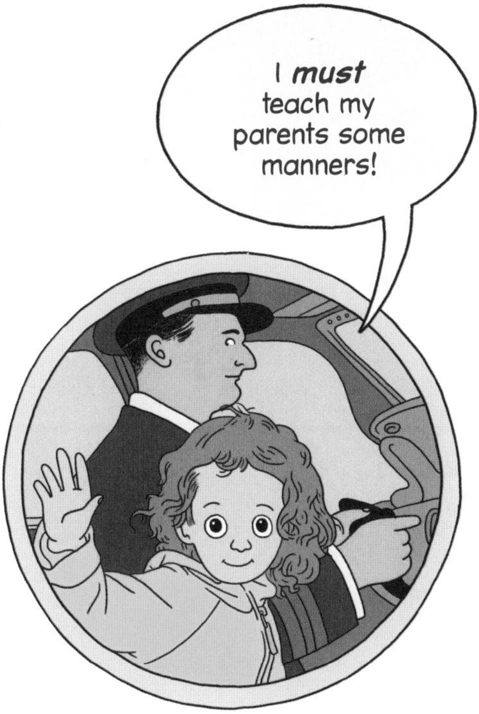
I *must* teach my parents some manners!

ABOUT THE AUTHOR

RUTU MODAN'S graphic novel, *Exit Wounds*, won the Eisner Award in 2008 and has been translated into 12 languages. And even though Rutu has received many awards for illustrating other authors' books, this is the first children's book she has written as well as drawn.

This book is a collaboration: When she was a child, Rutu liked ketchup so much she used to eat it with everything, even with cookies, or straight from the bottle (but only when her parents were not around). Then when Rutu's daughter, Michal, was young, she had very bad table manners. Rutu told her: "How badly you eat! What would you do if the Queen invited you to dine at the palace?" Michal answered very seriously: "Well! It just so happens that the Queen is a VERY good friend of mine, and she told me that I eat perfectly."

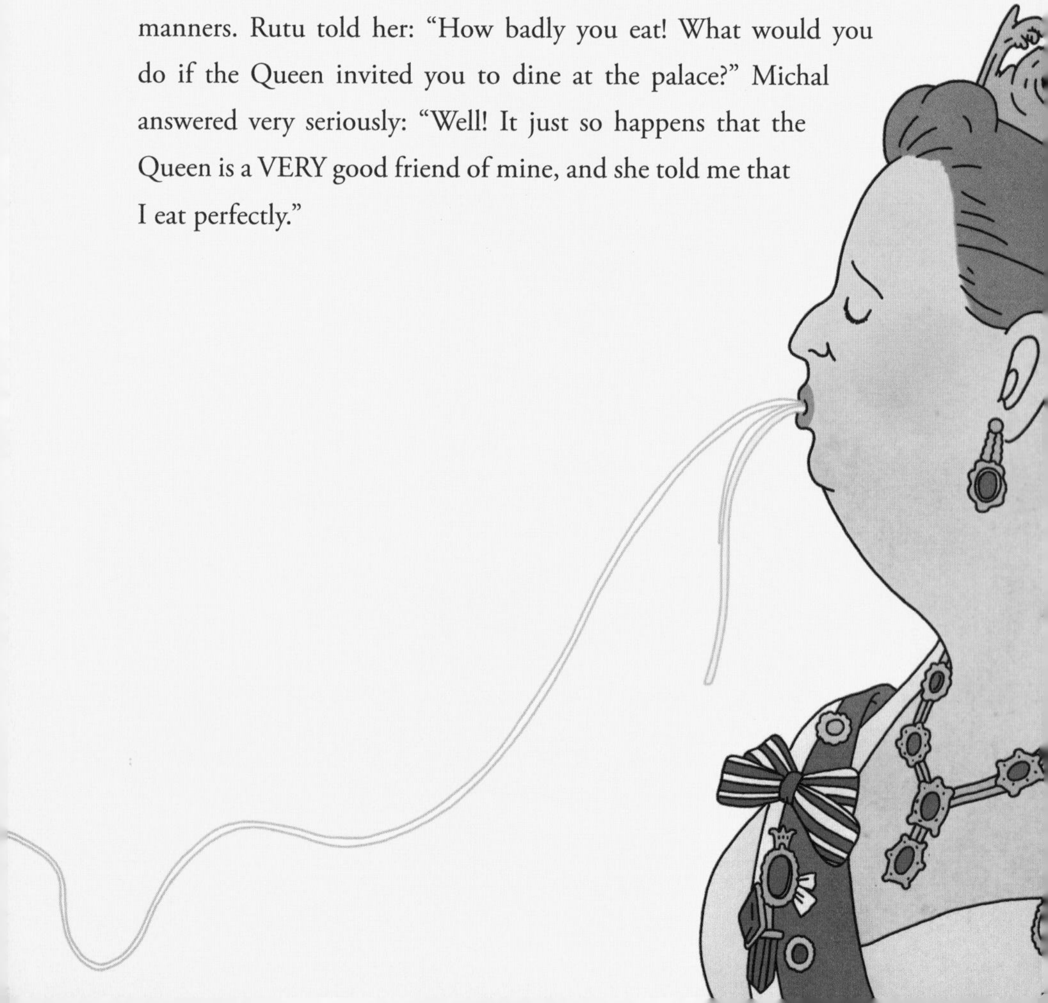

HOW TO "TOON INTO READING"
in a few simple steps:

Our goal is to get kids reading—and we know kids LOVE comics. We publish award-winning early readers in comics form for elementary and early middle school, and present them in three levels.

1 FIND THE RIGHT BOOK

Veteran teacher Cindy Rosado tells what makes a good book for beginning and struggling readers alike: "A vetted vocabulary, plenty of picture clues, repetition, and a clear and compelling story. Also, the book shouldn't be too easy—or the reader won't learn, but neither should it be too hard—or he or she may get discouraged."

The TOON INTO READING!™ program is designed for beginning readers and works wonders with reluctant readers.

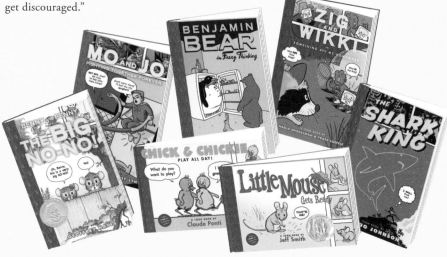

BENJAMIN BEAR in Fuzzy Thinking
MO AND JO FIGHTING TOGETHER FOREVER
ZIG AND WIKKI
THE SHARK KING
BENNY AND PENNY THE BIG NO-NO!
CHICK & CHICKIE PLAY ALL DAY!
What do you want to play?
A TOON BOOK BY Claude Ponti
Little Mouse Gets Ready
A TOON BOOK BY Jeff Smith

2 TAKE TIME WITH SILENT PANELS

Comics use panels to mark time, and silent panels count. Look and "read" even when there are no words. Often, humor is all in the timing!

KNOCK! KNOCK!
TRICK OR TREAT!

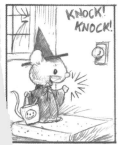

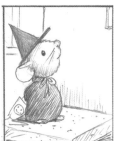

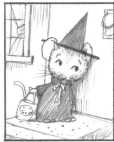

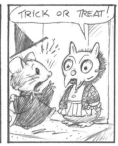

3 GUIDE YOUNG READERS

What works?

Keep your fingertip <u>below</u> the character that is speaking.

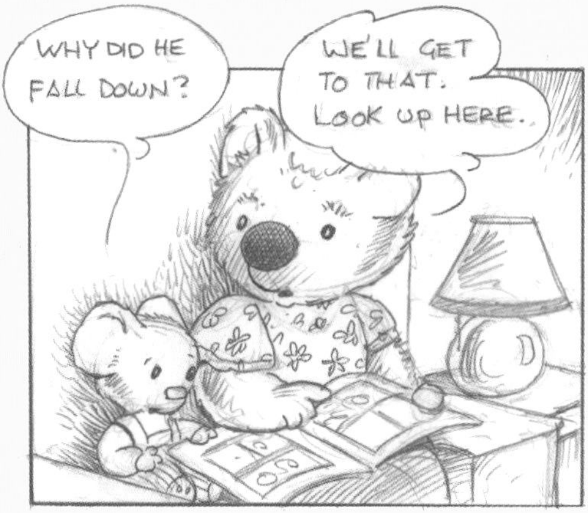
WHY DID HE FALL DOWN?
WE'LL GET TO THAT. LOOK UP HERE.

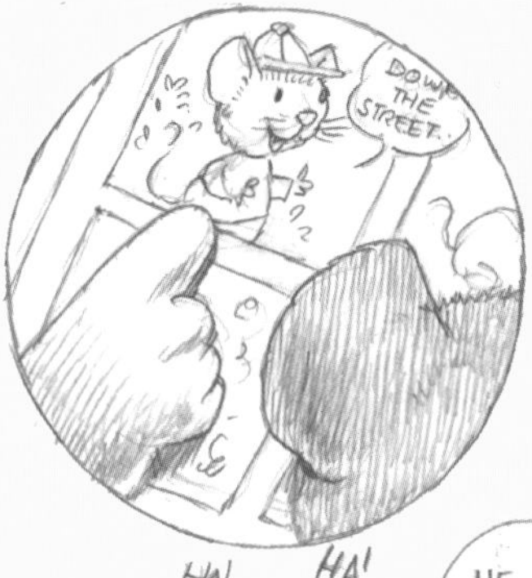
THE STREET.

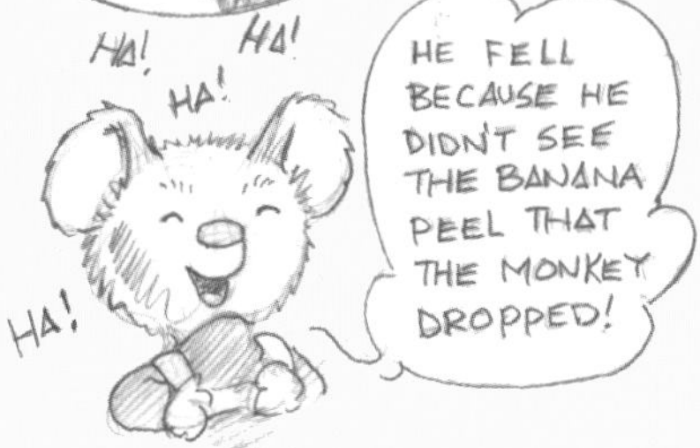
HA! HA!
HA!
HA!
HE FELL BECAUSE HE DIDN'T SEE THE BANANA PEEL THAT THE MONKEY DROPPED!

4 LET THE PICTURES TELL THE STORY

In a comic, you can often read the story even if you don't know all the words. Encourage young readers to tell you what's happening based on the facial expressions and body language.

5 GET OUT THE CRAYONS

Kids see the hand of the author in a comic and it makes them want to tell their own stories. Encourage them to talk, write and draw!

Get kids talking, and you'll be surprised at how perceptive they are about pictures.

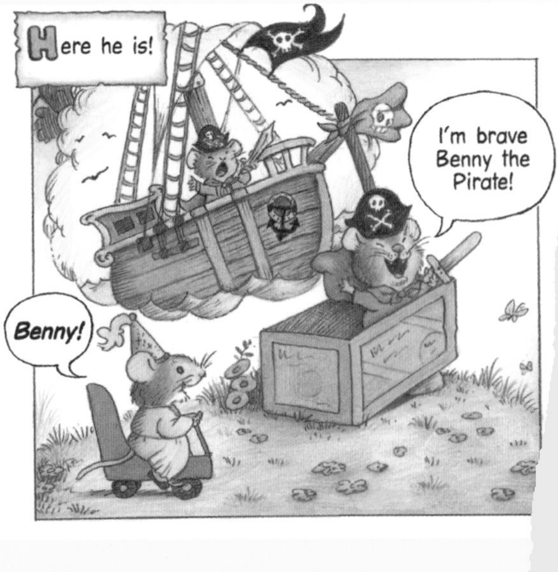
Here he is!
I'm brave Benny the Pirate!
Benny!

6 LET THEM GUESS

Comics provide a large amount of context for the words, so let young readers make informed guesses, and don't over-correct. In this panel, the artist shows a pirate ship, two pirate hats, and two pirate flags the first time the word "PIRATE" is introduced.